"If you're going to interrupt my wedding, at least have the decency to tell me why."

"You know why I'm interrupting. God, you're not going to claim some sort of mistaken identity, are you? Or that you have a twin brother?"

"I assure you, the only person making a ridiculous spectacle of themselves is you, Miss...?" Another hushed murmur went through the crowd, as if they weren't used to hearing this timbre. As if this version of the man who was familiar to her was a stranger to them.

Could it be? Surely not...? Surely, this man who could raise and raze dynasties at will hadn't taken leave of his faculties? It was unconscionable.

But then it would also explain every second of his absence. Would explain the complete vanishing act. Would explain why the man she'd never dreamed would walk away from the one thing he treasured most—his beloved company—had abandoned it so conclusively and entirely.

"My name is Imogen Callahan Diamandis. Yours is Zephyr Diamandis. And in case you're still confused, I'm your wife!"

Maya Blake's hopes of becoming a writer were born when she picked up her first romance at thirteen. Little did she know her dream would come true! Does she still pinch herself every now and then to make sure it's not a dream? Yes, she does! Feel free to pinch her, too, via Twitter, Facebook or Goodreads! Happy reading!

Books by Maya Blake

Harlequin Presents

The Greek's Hidden Vows
Reclaimed for His Royal Bed

Brothers of the Desert

Their Desert Night of Scandal
His Pregnant Desert Queen

The Notorious Greek Billionaires

Claiming My Hidden Son
Bound by My Scandalous Pregnancy

Ghana's Most Eligible Billionaires

Bound by Her Rival's Baby
A Vow to Claim His Hidden Son

Visit the Author Profile page
at Harlequin.com for more titles.

Maya Blake

THE GREEK'S
FORGOTTEN MARRIAGE

Recycling programs
for this product may
not exist in your area.

ISBN-13: 978-1-335-58430-4

The Greek's Forgotten Marriage

Harlequin Enterprises ULC
22 Adelaide St. West, 41st Floor
Toronto, Ontario M5H 4E3, Canada
www.Harlequin.com

Printed in U.S.A.

THE GREEK'S
FORGOTTEN MARRIAGE

CHAPTER ONE

THE TINY CHURCH at the top of the hill was cute beyond words.

Efemia, the Greek island tucked away in a forgotten corner of the Aegean, was the kind of place tourists cooed over and excitedly photographed from the outside while, inside, pious grandmothers clutched their rosaries and whispered fervent prayers.

It was the very last place Imogen Callahan expected to be. Certainly the last place she'd anticipated her frantic search would culminate. For several stunned seconds, she stared up at the dazzling whitewashed, blue-domed structure, with the slightly unevenly spaced windows, the sparkling Aegean its picture-perfect backdrop, still unable to comprehend what her private investigator had discovered. Unable to comprehend what was about to happen within the sacred walls. If indeed the report was true.

Had he gone insane? Or was this another of those multi-tiered games he excelled at, where most participants didn't even know they were playing until it was too late, and he was striding away with his prize?

Imogen firmed her lips as, from inside the chapel, the crescendo of voices sang the last refrain of a Greek hymn. She willed her hands not to shake as she mounted the last few steps, reached out and grasped the cool, solid aged iron handle.

Whatever game was going on, it was past time it came to an end. It had to, before she went out of her mind. She'd spent far too many nights tossing and turning, the unknown eating an acid path through her chest.

Through her life.

Well, no more.

With a deep breath in, she wrenched the heavy door open, the sound of old hinges creaking in the silence making her cringe.

Sunlight slanted through stained-glass windows, bathing the small congregation in streaks of vivid colour. But the couple at the head of the altar were shrouded in muted shadow. That didn't stop her from gaining an impression of a tall, towering frame and broad shoulders, of sculptured features and a penetrating gaze whose force was immediate, laser sharp and commanding as he turned towards her.

As was far too predictable with this man…*if it was him*… She shivered in bone-deep awareness, the overpowering magnetism that was never far already eddying around her. Then she grew impatient with herself for doing so. It could be a stranger for all she knew. Another dead end.

Still…she needed to make sure. Nothing but absolute certainty would suffice.

So she forced herself to step forward through the doors. To clear her throat. To tilt her chin and aim her gaze at the priest who stood in a circle of light two steps above the couple, his hands folded benevolently in front of his robes.

'I'm not sure what's going on here. But this farce needs to end. Right now,' Imogen announced, tone firm, intent unwavering.

The shocked silence, broken almost immediately by fervent whispering, then gawping expressions that ensued were like a scene from the *telenovelas* her late grandmother had loved to devour. Except this wasn't make believe. This was her *life*.

She swallowed again as stunned expressions began to grow disapproving, then downright hostile, her words and the click of her heels as she advanced commanding every gaze.

At the top of the aisle, the priest frowned, his own gaze turning less benevolent the closer she got.

Imogen didn't need to look down to be reminded of what she looked like.

The blow-out hairdo she'd let her stylist talk her into had got even wilder as the hours grew smaller, the heavier than usual make-up dramatising her every feature as a precursor to highlighting every emerald sequin of her thigh-skimming dress in the blinding sunlight, the red-soled heels looking positively indecent in the small, hallowed space.

She knew she looked completely out of place in a church, but she refused to be embarrassed by her appearance.

She'd been at a nightclub in Athens when she'd received the text from the PI.

A rare occurrence in and of itself because she'd rarely socialised in the past ten months. Returning to her apartment to change hadn't even occurred to her. The visceral need to rush here, *to know*, had been all-encompassing.

Feeling every inch of the congregation's judgment, she wanted to blurt that this wasn't how she usually dressed; that she wasn't one for short, barely there dresses that flaunted more skin than fabric. That she was more at home in power suits than cocktail dresses. But she didn't owe anyone an explanation of how she lived her life these days. Not since she'd finally offered one last sacrifice and stepped out from under her father's thumb.

Instead, she raised her chin, boldly met censorious gaze after censorious gaze until one by one they began to fall away. Of course, the gazes fell to her skimpy, thigh-skimming hem, bare legs and sky-high Louboutins, especially when she started to move towards the couple who were also turned towards her, as frozen as the rest of the congregation who were now beginning to whisper louder in Greek.

The priest skirted the couple and stepped towards her, arms outstretched as if shielding them from whatever harm he imagined Imogen intended to do to them.

Rapid-fire words were launched at her.

She shook her head, her long dark hair falling about her shoulders as she carried on down the aisle. 'I'm afraid I don't speak Greek. But I sincerely hope you understand English because, like I said, you need to stop this...whatever this is before you make a serious mistake.'

'And what mistake would that be?'

Imogen froze mid-step, finally brought to a halt by the cool query that didn't come from the priest but from the prospective groom.

Because...*dear God*.

That voice.

Deep. Rasping. Commanding. *Hypnotic*.

It had sent CEOs and minions alike scurrying for cover. It'd sent her own father into a downward spiral that had ultimately resulted in Imogen being offered up as a completely unwilling sacrifice.

It'd sent her alternately sobbing and raging when its owner had drawled his refusal to listen to reason. When he'd dispassionately rejected her every imploration to reconsider the heinous price he'd demanded from her family.

In her darkest nights over the last ten months, she'd wondered why she was so tormented by the notion that she'd never hear his voice again when she should've been relieved that she was finally, *finally* free.

Hearing it now, she knew she'd only been fooling herself. Somehow, she'd known she'd never be free of it, of *him*, until she took definitive steps to make it so.

It was why she'd never given up trying to find him.

And now she had—

'I asked you a question. If you're going to interrupt my wedding, at least have the decency to tell me why.'

My wedding.

Had he gone mad? Or did power truly corrupt absolutely as the saying went? Because this was truly next-level insanity. This was hubris above and beyond what even she'd imagined him capable of. And he'd shown her a lot during their short, intensely charged time together.

Before he'd vanished off the face of the earth.

She took one last step and the angle of the light changed, throwing him into sharp, dramatic relief. Imogen inhaled sharply, right before her breath locked in her lungs.

After so many dead ends, she hadn't, deep down, believed that this new lead would pan out. Hadn't believed that the man she'd been searching for had been right here in Greece all along. In this backwater village tucked away out of sight, where the Internet was sketchy to the point of non-existent, and indoor plumbing was considered a luxury, according to her handsomely paid PI.

Was she missing some vital angle? What the hell was he playing at?

A softly murmured question in Greek made Imogen turn her attention to the woman at his side. Tucked under his protective arm.

Something caught tighter in Imogen's chest as several uncharitable thoughts flitted through her head.

Was she some sort of witch? Or, worse yet, considering they were in the very birthplace of Greek mythology, a *siren*? Because none of this made sense.

She took a step closer, to get a better view of her, then froze when the man stepped forward to block her way.

The protective arm he kept around the woman sent sharp darts through her Imogen didn't want to acknowledge. So what if he was protective of this woman? Theirs had never been that sort of relationship. It'd been forged within the cold, clinical walls of the boardroom, finalised in an even colder civil court in Athens. And in light of what had come after, that was where it'd end.

Soon, she silently prayed.

She'd put her life on hold for not one but two men—her father, and this man. Simply because she'd been born a woman. *Enough.*

'You know why I'm interrupting. God, you're not going to claim some sort of mistaken identity, are you? Or that you have a twin brother?'

Surprisingly, a whisper of uncertainty flickered in his eyes before his jaw clenched and he exhaled with visible displeasure. 'Not that I'm aware of,' he said.

'Then can we dispense with this façade?'

'I assure you, the only strange activity going on here currently is your uninvited presence here, Miss…?'

Imogen started. 'Seriously?' She cast a look around, clocked the avid gazes of the congregation. Forced herself to look closer, to see if there was anyone critical she'd missed. Any of the notable people of industry who'd tended to gravitate towards this man's power like moths to a flame. Anyone who could explain why this ruse was necessary. When she didn't, when all she saw were villagers dressed simply, with openly curious stares and none of the cut-throat machinations she was used to seeing in the business world, she faced him again. 'If you're pranking me, I assure you, this isn't funny in the least.'

'And I assure you, the only person making a ridiculous spectacle of themselves is you, *Miss…?*' The second pointed query came sharper now, that imperious tone she was well familiar with rumbling through the silence. Another hushed murmur went through the crowd, as if they weren't used to hearing this timbre. As if this version of the man who was familiar to her was a stranger to them.

Familiar.

Stranger.

Imogen's breath caught as possibilities bombarded her brain.

Dear God…

Could it be? Surely not…? Surely, this man who could raise and raze dynasties at will hadn't taken leave of his faculties? It was unconscionable.

But then it would also explain every second of his absence. Would explain the complete vanishing act. Would explain why the man she'd never dreamed would have walked away from the one thing he treasured most—his beloved company— had abandoned it so conclusively and entirely.

Every morning she'd woken up and wondered what he was playing at.

Where he was playing it.

Whether *she* would eventually go out of her mind with not knowing.

The possibility that this was a deliberate act shook through her.

But no. It didn't seem possible.

So she took one last step and stared into the eyes of the man whose face and name were imprinted on her so indelibly, she knew it would take a superhuman feat to remove them.

'My name is Imogen Callahan Diamandis. Yours is Zephyr Diamandis.' And just in case he still doubted her or intended to keep up this puzzling game, she raised her left hand, where he had slipped the obscene diamond that matched his name onto her finger in a sterile room as different from this charming chapel as night from day. 'And in case you're still confused, I'm your wife!'

Zephyr Diamandis.

The name was unashamedly Greek.

Arrogantly and pompously so, some might even say. A world removed from the pedestrian Yiannis he'd settled on when he woke up in the strange bed ten months ago.

Shock immobilised him as his brain searched frantically to parse through the bombshell just detonated at his feet. But like every time he attempted it, a dull throb commenced at his temples. As if urging him to let go. To forget.

Zephyr Diamandis.

It was as alien to him as Yiannis.

Yiannis With-No-Last-Name.

That was what his soon-to-be *yiayia* by marriage had laughingly called him for months after he was welcomed into Petros's small family.

While the name hadn't quite settled on him as he'd secretly wished it would, he'd accepted it. Because really, he'd had very little to call his own back then, save for the tattered clothes he'd been found in. And the fact that he spoke the language and must be Greek.

His life had improved somewhat since then, however. Now he boasted a handful of friends, cordial neighbours and even a job helping Petros manage his ten fishing vessels. Altogether, he was content enough—although was complete contentment ever achievable?—to have finally given in to the gentle but firm nudges from Petros to make an honest woman of his daughter.

Enough for him to set aside—for now at least—the quest to discover his past.

As Petros had reasoned, if he was important to anyone out there in the wide world, surely the local police force—although it was a stretch to call the single policeman who settled all squabbles at the village taverna a *force*—would've found something by now?

He shifted beneath the itch between his shoulder blades, the thin inner voice that mocked him for not pushing harder. For ignoring the quiet urgency that dogged him at night.

'Yiannis?'

He turned to the woman enclosed within his arm, a little startled that he'd forgotten all about her in the aftermath of this stranger...this scantily dressed, fearless and offensive, stunning... *beauty* who proclaimed herself his wife.

Whose bright green eyes held both defiance and censure. Whose overfull lips were the most sensual lips he'd ever seen. Whose lustrous chestnut locks he wanted to sink his fingers—

Theós...he wasn't seriously contemplating one woman's lips when he was standing before an altar, minutes away from marrying another, was he?

Should he thank this woman...whoever she was—because he still wasn't convinced this wasn't some cosmic joke, perhaps an overextension of the beer-filled bachelor's party the village men had thrown him two nights ago—for saving him from committing bigamy?

A small hand touched his chest and he refocused on Thea, his almost-bride.

Her face held wariness and confusion, much like the emotions churning through him.

'His name isn't Yiannis,' the woman—his wife—said.

Flicking a glance at her, he watched her nostrils flare in jealousy and felt a punch of something— hot and vibrant and puzzlingly satisfying—inside him.

What the hell?

Was he…glad that this woman was jealous of Thea?

Ever the thinker, as Petros had also laughingly labelled him, he placed himself in the woman's position. Then felt a distinctly unpleasant emotion churn in his gut.

Ne, he would be vastly disgruntled too, if he discovered his wife was marrying another man.

But…he only had *her* word for it.

'I am your husband?' Why did that question punch something hot and heavy through his veins?

'Yes,' the woman… Imogen…responded, although something shook in her voice he couldn't quite recognise.

The throb at his temple stepped up another notch as he watched her. 'Prove it,' he drawled eventually.

Her eyes widened and, again, something snagged in his midriff. Her eyes were enchanting, reflecting shards of the multicoloured light streaming through the windows. For some absurd reason, he wanted to step closer, look deeper into those aquamarine depths.

'What?'

He forced himself to continue the entirely rational demand. Allowed himself to rake his gaze over her body to prove his point. 'Prove that this isn't some prank *you* are pulling. We get tourists like you on the isle all the time, looking for…unsavoury ways to amuse themselves. Prove you're not on here to extend whatever *dare* you've been chosen to play.'

Her jaw sagged, her chest heaving in disbelief. 'Are you joking?'

Her accent was foreign. American or Canadian—although he couldn't pinpoint exactly how he knew that. And he was a little taken aback with how alluring he found it. How much he wanted to step closer, press his thumb to that luscious lower, pouting lip.

He tightened his gut, pressing his hand over Thea's to gather a semblance of control. To relocate the integrity that Petros and Yiayia had both praised him for.

Again he watched her gaze flick to the gesture, watched her green eyes flash for a second before she corralled it.

Interesting…

Why would she want to hide that emotion from him? He was absolutely certain he wouldn't throttle his emotions if he were watching her being claimed by—

Enough.

'Surely, you didn't just expect me to take you at your word?' he said as Petros, the man who would've been his father-in-law by now if they hadn't been interrupted, rose from his seat and joined them.

The woman's mouth closed and opened. 'I'm not…' She stopped and shook her head. 'This isn't a prank, believe me.'

He flicked up an eyebrow, and watched, far too fascinated, as she plucked a phone from a minuscule handbag whose strap was slung across her body, prompting Yiannis… Zephyr…to become aware of her full, perky breasts.

A sleek phone emerged but before she could produce the evidence he sought, Petros stepped forward.

'What my son is too polite to say is that we have…visitors like you far too frequently in our village, hoping to bask in a slice of our admittedly simple lives, so they can go and boast about it to their friends. What is it you want, exactly, miss?'

She shook her head. 'Your son?' she echoed, ignoring the rest of Petros's query. Then her gaze slanted to him, a look in her eyes that winked out far too quickly for Yiannis to decipher. 'This isn't your father.'

His heart jumped, the thirst for knowledge almost making him blurt out a demand for her to elaborate. To tell him everything she knew about him. He bit his lip just in time. He hadn't ascertained that this woman wasn't toying with him; that she wasn't everything Petros was accusing her of.

Petros waved her response away, triggering a curious dissatisfaction in Yiannis. 'He's my son in all the ways that count. Now, if you've finished entertaining yourself, we have a ceremony to finish. Unless you truly have this proof to show us?'

The woman looked from Petros to him. Then, with another defiant look that sent yet another hot poker of lust through him, she flicked on her phone.

His breath strangled in his chest, his free hand bunching at his side as her fingers flew over the screen. Only for those kissable lips to purse. 'I don't have any cell reception.'

He smiled to hide the searing disappointment and acute hollowness in his stomach. 'You don't need the Internet to access photos on your phone, Miss Diamandis. Are you saying that you don't have a single photo of us together on your camera roll?' he taunted.

He followed the path of heat that rushed into

her face before her gaze fell from his. He caught the tail of wariness and his insides stiffened further. There was something else going on here, something besides her outrageous announcement.

He wanted to catch her chin and direct her gaze to his, but he'd allowed himself to be distracted by this woman for long enough.

'It's *Mrs* Diamandis,' she said, another peculiar look flickering over her smooth, satin-like skin. 'Or Miss Callahan if you prefer to use my maiden name.'

He didn't prefer it. If they truly shared a connection, he would never resort to her previous name. The clutch of possessiveness made him press his lips together.

'And as Petros said, we have a marriage ceremony to finish. Admit you stormed in here to get a top-up of whatever titivation you were up to last night,' he said, unable to stop his gaze from trailing over her again, swallowing discreetly at the sight of her spectacular, bare legs. 'And I will let you walk away with an apology.'

Her chin rose, green fire swirling in her eyes. 'And if I don't?'

A few breaths caught in the audience, the few who understood English hearing the taunt in her tone.

'Yiannis, please take care of this,' Thea urged softly in Greek.

He stared down into her gentle face. Petros's only child was modestly beautiful, her features draped in that touch of melancholy that had clung to her after the loss of her fiancé three years ago. He wasn't sure whether it was her delicateness or that melancholy that had kept him at arm's length, even during their very short engagement.

Whatever it was, it'd never prompted him to even kiss or take things further with her.

While he hadn't given much thought about the type of woman he preferred, Thea definitely lacked the daring and feistiness of the woman claiming to be his wife.

He grimaced inwardly at the comparison but admitted that, as much as he liked Thea Angelos, this had never been a love match. They'd drifted into a friendship encouraged by Petros, a man who had seen a chance to perpetuate his family and determinedly stoked it. And he, Yiannis, had gone along with it because he'd felt as if he owed Petros something after the man had saved his life.

'*Ne*,' he responded now. This interruption had gone on long enough. 'If you don't, I'll have you escorted out.'

He turned and nodded to the priest, who breathed a sigh of relief and climbed back onto the dais. Before he could open his mouth, the woman's husky voice froze proceedings. Again.

'Your superyacht, which you named *Ophelia*

I, after your mother, is anchored a mile offshore,' she blurted. 'If you don't believe me, just step outside. You can see it from the top of this hill. You have a staff of thirty-five manning it, and you've known the pilot since you were twenty-one years old. You were on board the yacht when you fell over the side and were presumed drowned ten months ago. Every single person on that vessel can corroborate who you are. Or you can go ahead and commit bigamy. Your choice.'

He stiffened. Not at the announcement that he was wealthy enough to own a superyacht, but at the acute sensation that cut through him at her words. He couldn't deny she had the timing right. As she did the 'presumed drowned' part. Because he'd been in serious danger of drowning when Petros and his men had fished him out of the ocean.

But there was something else.

The knowledge that this supposed affluence surely came with responsibility.

Clout. Power. Dynamism. *More*.

All facets of himself he'd sensed echoing just out of reach. Facets he'd suppressed because it'd made him seem ungrateful for the open-hearted generosity Petros and his family had shown him. Facets he'd felt pulling at him in his unguarded moments when he should've been basking in the wealth of affection and warmth but had instead felt...adrift. Grateful, yes, but...*diminished.*

He felt it strain within him now, tethers of this life binding him when he wanted...*no*, was *destined* to be free.

Or was he being fanciful? Reaching for something his faulty psyche was tricking him into believing he needed?

All because of this woman?

A raised murmur went through the crowd as he hesitated. A few people rose from the pew and drifted towards the window, eager to verify for themselves.

When he heard the first gasp, a knot twisted painfully in his gut, then slowly began to unravel, loosening the first of many leashes.

'Yiannis,' Petros uttered his name cautiously.

But he knew...deep in his bones, *he knew*, this was the moment he'd waited ten long months for.

As if he sensed what was coming, Petros shook his head and narrowed his eyes at their intruder. 'You claim to know this man. Tell me what he was wearing the last time you saw him,' he demanded, unfamiliar hostility stiffening his shoulders.

'He was wearing a sea-green shirt with long sleeves and light brown cargo pants. He also had a thin leather bracelet with a titanium clasp but that could've been lost.'

Petros exhaled in defeat and the fire went out of him. Because the description was accurate, even if the state of those clothes had been beyond rescue. The leather bracelet had deteriorated within weeks, and Yiannis had had to dispose of it after intense examination showed it bore no signs of who he was.

Regret scythed through him as he glanced at Petros. 'I'm sorry, old friend.' *I need to know.*

The older man's features clenched, possibly from being addressed as friend instead of the *pateras* he'd been urging Yiannis to call him lately. Or possibly because he, too, knew the time had come.

Most of their guests were at the window now, and he was a little thankful for it, because it gave him the privacy he needed.

But staring into Thea's face, he smiled wryly at the faint relief in her eyes.

No, she wasn't over her dead fiancé. And she proved it with how easily she accepted his decision when she stepped back from him, into her father's waiting arms.

Yiannis... Zephyr—if this stranger was to be believed—turned and faced the woman who'd fallen silent after making the bold announcement.

Now he was free, he was even more taken aback by the punch of hot attraction in his gut, by the rise of his manhood after ten long months

of disinterest in carnal pleasure. This woman—
his wife—was his.

His to kiss. To touch. *To claim.*

But first… 'If this turns out to be an elaborate
joke, Miss Callahan, be assured that you will live
to regret it.'

CHAPTER TWO

IMOGEN KEPT HER gaze on the horizon and away from the man who had refused to take a seat on the launch transporting them to the fast-approaching yacht and instead stood with feet planted apart, one hand braced on the side of the sleek vessel.

The man whose piercing, narrow-eyed gaze swung metronomically between the yacht and her face, oftentimes staying for several nerve-tingling seconds before retreating.

She didn't know if whatever information he was seeking had been evident in her face. And she wasn't sure she wanted to know. Her emotions were still twanging wildly from what had taken place in that church. And, goodness, what had taken place after had been equally astonishing.

Once Zephyr had decided he would investigate her claims for himself, nothing would sway him from it.

His departure hadn't been without distress for those left behind. For Petros especially. She hadn't needed to understand Greek to know the old man had implored Zeph to reconsider, nor did she need a body-language expert to decipher the scathing looks he'd thrown Imogen while he did so. The elderly woman had wept quietly, and she'd been the one Zeph had spent most time with, speaking gently but firmly to her until she'd pressed a hand to his hard cheek in forgiving understanding.

As for the woman he'd intended to marry, she'd only worn a solemn, worried expression mostly directed at her father and the old woman Imogen guessed was her grandmother. The looks she'd cast Zeph weren't filled with censure or heartbreak, making Immie wonder—with something eerily akin to relief she didn't want to fully explore—whether their intended marriage had been one of convenience just as hers was.

All in all, it'd taken less than an hour for Zephyr to cut ties with the life he'd known for ten months. Immie couldn't say she was surprised. The man she'd had no choice but to be tied to was nothing if not ruthlessly efficient.

He hadn't spoken a word since they left Efemia—and his almost-bride and her family—behind.

The whole trip took less than five minutes, but by the time that gaze pinned her one more time and he held out his hand to help her off the boat, Imogen was a bag of nerves. Enough for her to hesitate before she slid her hand into his. Enough to suppress a wild gasp that shook into her throat at the first true and meaningful contact she'd had with her husband since he slid that cold diamond onto her finger in that sterile room in Athens almost two years ago.

Then, she'd been too distraught by the circumstances of how she'd become the sacrificial lamb for her family to accommodate the electrifying effect he seemed to effortlessly conjure out of her.

Sure, she'd been aware of the devastatingly handsome Zephyr Diamandis, the man who'd dated more than a handful of the most beautiful women in the world. Which had also begged the question, why her? The answer had been too glaringly obvious to dismiss—revenge. That knowledge had pushed everything else into the background.

Now she'd seen him again, solid and alive and, hell, *thriving*, the recollection of why this man hated her bubbled forth now.

Revenge born of the age-old demon that often sprang from the wells of thwarted regard or respect. In their families' case—and in Zephyr Diamandis's eyes—it'd been disregard for fairness.

Her grandfather and father's blithe disregard for the deal they'd struck with Zeph's grandfather had driven his family into bankruptcy, a fact Imogen's father still refused to fully accept responsibility for even now. Even after offering her, his only child, as penance to save *himself* from destitution.

But she'd done her homework, enough to know the shocking consequences her family's actions had produced.

The Diamandises had lost everything after her father and grandfather failed to honour the terms of the shipping deal Zeph's family had sunk their every last euro into.

Overnight, they'd gone from being on the brink of indecent wealth to being destitute. Pariahs who'd been vilified in Athens. His grandfather had suffered a heart attack very soon after that. And one by one, his father, then his mother had also been lost, working themselves into an early death while attempting to salvage what little they'd been left with, leaving an embittered young boy behind. A boy who'd been thrown into the foster-care system and effectively left to bring himself up, steeped in the knowledge that one family—the Callahans—had been responsible for the drastic course his life had taken.

So no, she wasn't surprised that this man hadn't touched her since he'd draped the millstone of his name around her neck and then estranged himself from her.

Now, however, she couldn't discard the sensations of tiny fireworks he evoked with his touch as their palms slid together. As his strong fingers curled around hers, firm and masculine, to help her onto the lower deck. As midnight-blue eyes stared forcefully and blatantly into hers, ruthlessly excavating her every secret.

Reminding her that a different reality was setting in.

Zephyr. Zeph.

Her long-lost husband was back. And he'd lost his memory. Apparently.

God, she still couldn't believe she'd found him.

Alive and well. Powerfully masculine and even more handsome…

And staring at her mouth as if…as if…

She sucked in a deep, composure-craving breath as the staff, lined up beside the pilot, and wearing looks of shock and muted elation, watched their employer step aboard the boat he'd disappeared off ten long months ago.

Alongside the shock, she also saw wide-eyed surprise. The same emotion unravelling through her at the transformation in the formidable, forbidding man she'd known for the last two years.

Because for his departure from the little hamlet he'd resided in since he went missing, Zeph hadn't chosen a suit or even a pair of trousers and a button-down shirt. Instead, the multibillionaire who could shift fiscal landscapes as easily as a gardener turned soil had changed into a pair of khaki shorts and a white T-shirt.

For a man who she'd never seen dressed any way but formally—courtesy of the exclusive dozen bespoke tailors spread across three continents at his beck and call—it'd been a shock to see him in shorts, a T-shirt, and *flip-flops*. Imogen was sure the Zeph of old wouldn't have known what flip-flops were if a pair had jumped out at him.

And even more shocking was the fact that... Immie liked this informal side of him.

More than liked.

She dragged her gaze from his mile-wide shoulders and the muscles—much thicker than the streamlined sleekness he'd sported before his disappearance—stretching beneath the thin cotton, past the strong throat and the wisps of silky hair peeking up from the neckline, to the lush brown locks ruffling in the slight breeze, and the way he casually wove his tanned fingers through them as he greeted his staff.

With a smile.

Good heavens. At this rate, she was sure she'd expire from astonishment before noon.

Titos, the pilot of the *Ophelia I*, broke into excited Greek chatter, a suspicious sheen in his eyes that looked like tears as he pumped his boss's hand in greeting.

Zeph responded in Greek before greeting his other staff, leaving awed, blinking staff in his wake.

When, after several minutes in conversation,

the head steward herded them away—following her firm request that for now Zeph's reappearance was to be kept confidential—her breath caught all over again when Zeph turned to her, the remnants of his smile still in place.

'Is something the matter?' he rasped.

And she realised she was gawping at him. 'I... you're smiling,' she blurted before she could stop herself.

A shade of that smile disappeared. Immie bit her tongue as his eyes narrowed a second later.

'You say that as if you're surprised.'

She shivered at the cool query in that observation. Cleared her throat as she thought of how to respond. Hadn't she read somewhere that volunteering unguarded information to amnesia patients could be detrimental?

'Miss Callahan?'

She bristled. Then immediately felt irritated with herself for doing so. Wasn't this what she ultimately wanted? Wasn't this why she'd searched high and low and under every rock for this man, driven by a visceral instinct she couldn't deny? Instinct that insisted that he was alive? So she could find him—despite the authorities and his board of directors urging her to have him declared dead—and draw a line one way or another under the past two years and reclaim her life? Her independence? To return to being Immie Callahan and not Imogen Diamandis, trophy wife of one of the wealthiest, most influential men on earth?

Yes, but his calling her by her maiden name was making a specific point. One she didn't appreciate.

She raised her chin. 'If you're attempting to cast doubt on the fact that we're married by using my maiden name, you're wasting your time.'

'I may not remember who I am, but I know not to take everything I'm told at face value.'

This was the Zeph she remembered. The terrifying Greek shipping tycoon and financier who could make grown men quake in their boots. Why that made something heavy inside her plummet, she refused to examine. 'What reason would I have to lie to you?'

'The same reason you're holding yourself so stiffly. The reason everyone around here seems pleased to see me except you.' Silk and danger. Those were the two components of his voice. And they sent a different shiver down her spine.

Because he'd spoken to her like that before his disappearance. Just her. No one else.

Whether he remembered it or not.

'Would you care to elaborate as to why that is?' he pressed.

She attempted a calm and composed shrug. 'I'm concerned about your well-being. This must be all new and…different from what you've been used to these last ten months. Maybe you should rest?'

That devastating smile broke through again and everything inside her roused to rude life. 'Again, I may not know myself as much as I'd wish to, but I'm confident I'm made of sterner stuff…*dear wife*.' He drawled the last two words out, his eyes pinned on her face.

So he probably didn't miss the unguarded gasp she tried to suppress. Then she rallied hard to get herself together. Answered the question still lingering in the air. 'Titos, your pilot… I don't speak Greek so I don't know if he reminded you of your childhood together. I'm sure he can corroborate whatever you need to know.'

His gaze didn't waver from her face for one instant. 'He seems a good man, but I'm not getting best friend and confidant vibes from him,' he replied.

And she couldn't refute that.

Zeph Diamandis has always been a lone wolf, an apex predator who ruled his world alone and with a titanium fist. Sure, he had dozens of business acquaintances and alliances, but true, lifelong friends? She hadn't come across a single one in the full year she'd been shoved into his orbit, then shackled to him in a game of pure retribution.

'Your hesitation tells me I'm right,' he drawled when she remained silent.

Immie cleared her throat. 'Okay, yes... I mean, no, you weren't best friends.'

'Then I'm certain there was a reason for it.'

The thinly veiled question sent alarm through her. Because suddenly, she wasn't sure if she wanted to provide him with vivid details of their relationships. Wasn't sure she wanted to tell him that far from being a conventional married couple, they'd been enemies, thrown together by the Diamandis code for retribution he'd vowed never to waver from.

The wrongs her family had done his had left a trail of devastation it'd taken Zephyr's father, then Zeph himself to right. And he'd risen from those ashes determined that a Callahan would pay.

That Callahan had been her.

He strode towards her, and she was reminded all over again—as if that phenomenon were ever far from her mind—how devastatingly handsome he was; how he could command a room without so much as speaking a word.

Even the wide, endless deck seemed like an enclosed cave as he pinned those laser-beam eyes on her. Eyes that made her intensely aware of every sensitive square inch of her skin. Aware of the tightening of her nipples and the sensitivity in her breasts.

What had he asked her again?

Friends. Relationships.

She licked her lips. 'I know you want answers, and we'll get around to it eventually—'

'*Ne*, I want answers,' he concurred, his Greek accent thickened. 'And you can start by telling me where you were last night. What you were doing going out dressed like that when your husband was missing.'

'Excuse me? How dare you?' Affront was immediate—and welcomed. She could hang on to that, suppress the other sensations he triggered in her. Sensations that reminded her far too vividly that she was a woman. Albeit a woman with negligible sexual experience. Because she didn't want to dwell on that hot, tight space between her legs that grew hotter with every scent of him she took into her nostrils, every glimpse of those sensual lips. Every ripple of those thick muscles. Every time her gaze fell on his callused hands and she imagined them on her body, deliciously chafing in their caresses.

'I'm not criticising your choice of attire, although I must admit to feeling a little…disgruntled that other men get to enjoy the sight of those spectacular legs.'

Her mouth dropped open in shock. Then she snapped it shut. 'Then…why? Because you…you sound…jealous.' The notion was absurd to speak aloud. Just as absurd as the spiky little thrill it sent through her!

'Do I? Is that as new a phenomenon as wanting to know my wife's whereabouts?'

As quickly as her ire had risen, it dissipated. Because again, he'd knocked the wind out of her with this staggering observation. The Zephyr Diamandis she knew hadn't exhibited an iota of emotion towards her, jealousy or otherwise.

Hell, she'd have been lucky if he'd shown anything other than stone-cold indifference. All he'd wanted was the convenient respectability of marriage to secure the biggest deal of his life—the acquisition of the multibillion-dollar conglomerate that was Avalon Inc.

Imogen wasn't sure how her father had known the ins and outs of the Diamandis negotiations with Avalon, or especially how he'd found out that Philip Avalon, the ninety-year-old magnate who had finally agreed to sell his company, had had one ultimate condition before agreeing to the deal with Zephyr. That the man acquiring his beloved company not be a 'philandering womaniser with more money than sense and no ties to keep him in line'.

Imogen would've laughed at the archaic concept, perhaps even pondered why a man as enlightened as Zeph Diamandis was agreeing to it, if she weren't the one directly in the crosshairs of that agreement. If her family's once thriving but now struggling company hadn't been at serious risk, too.

That the Avalon deal had included its subsidiary, Callahan Shipping, had been a minor incentive, but an incentive nevertheless because, in one fell swoop, he'd been able to deliver the sucker punch every Callahan family member had been bracing for for almost two decades. Zeph had acquired Avalon, and with it her beloved company, the company she'd earned a business and marketing degree for and had poured blood, sweat and tears into, despite every single deprecatory putdown from her father.

And in the months before his disappearance, Diamandis Shipping had become one of the largest individually owned companies in the world, making her husband one of the wealthiest, most influential men on the planet.

Did he even realise how powerful he was? This man dressed in shorts and a T-shirt who was asking about her activities as a *normal* run-of-the-mill husband who cared for his wife would?

Except there was nothing run-of-the-mill about the look he continued to level at her, the expectation of an answer heavy in the air and growing weightier by the second.

'If you must know, I was out with your...with the company's clients last night.'

His gaze raked over her once more, his nostrils flaring. 'And are you in the habit of regularly entertaining these clients outside office hours?'

She shrugged. 'Not often but…' She stopped, a touch of anger and disconsolation riling her anew as she was reminded of why she'd needed to act out of the ordinary. 'None of the other board members were available.' A very convenient result of every last one of them scattering to their various plush villas and summer homes and leaving her to handle these particularly demanding clients.

'And these clients, they were that important?'

'So far they've been…challenging, but yes, they are.' And the board had pulled rank over her, the youngest member, and despite her title as acting CEO in her husband's absence, the one most responsible.

It hadn't factored that she'd had a million other responsibilities to take care of. Plus a missing husband to find. They'd merely shrugged and told her if she cared that much about securing the Canadian brothers' business then she needed to step up.

Zeph's eyes narrowed as he no doubt attempted to read between the lines. Afraid that he'd do just that, that he'd see how much of a battle she'd had to fight to retain her seat on the all-male board, and how debasing she'd found their treatment of her, she rose and turned away, discarding the stilettos that were killing her feet before striding to the rail.

For several seconds, she let the sweet, mid-morning breeze wash over her. Then, when everything that had happened crowded in, reminding her that there were a million other things to take care of, least of which was announcing Zeph Diamandis's return from the dead to the world, she squared her shoulders and turned.

Only to gasp when she found him behind her, hands shoved in his pockets as he watched her. 'What…did you need something?'

'Other than the full picture I suspect you're not showing me?' he rasped, one eyebrow quirked upward.

'I don't know what you're talking about,' she hedged.

His lips pursed. 'Of course you do but I'll leave it alone, for now. Tell me, what was the outcome of this evening's entertainment?'

She breathed a sigh of relief to answer straightforwardly, choosing to bat away the horrendous hours she'd spent socialising with the twin Canadian brothers who took the *play harder* part of the saying to a whole new level. 'Somewhere around dawn, the terms of the deal were agreed. It's with our lawyers right now. Pending a green light from them, we'll sign a substantial supply contract with them later this week.'

Imogen wasn't sure what she'd expected. Indifference? Apathy? That clinical coldness he used to address her with.

The mixture of pride and fury that flashed through his eyes threw her for a loop. Before she could query it, he was speaking. 'While I congratulate you for getting the deal done—and I look forward to seeing the net result for myself—I find myself dissatisfied with the process.'

She shrugged, attempting not to take the criticism personally. 'For success to be guaranteed, execution is everything,' she muttered, still disturbed by his proximity and what it was doing to her equilibrium.

His eyes narrowed. 'Sounds like a talking-head quote. Anyone you know?'

'You. In a *Forbes* magazine article when you were named Man of the Year three years ago.'

Instead of basking in the accolade, as most would've, he sharpened his scrutiny even more. 'Are you testing me, *matia mou*?' he drawled. 'Perhaps you hold your reservation about my memory loss?'

She hadn't but, now he mentioned it, perhaps subconsciously she'd thrown his own words at him to attempt to elicit a response. Because an indifferent husband was one thing.

This new, equally enigmatic but emotionally expressive edition of Zephyr Diamandis was quite another.

Yiannis…no, Zeph—he needed to remember that he was no longer Yiannis the fisherman—watched her flush and do that gaze-avoiding thing that sent wariness shooting through him.

And yet it was that pink tongue slicking her lower lip that affected him more. Telling himself it was natural—after all, if they were married, the attraction was justified, wasn't it?—didn't quite ring true. Sure, he'd only just returned to this purported life he'd missed ten months of. And if the crew, who'd respectfully and almost reverently referred to him as Kyrios Diamandis were to be believed, he was their boss, the owner of this impressive vessel and a whole lot more assets in the great wide world.

But instinct blared wildly that he was missing a whole subset beneath the reality his mind was hiding from him. And in this moment, he couldn't seem to see beyond that.

'I don't think we should have any…um…in-depth conversations until you've been checked out medically,' she said, her glances starting out furtive, and then, as he watched her straighten her spine, meeting his boldly.

'I feel fine,' he dismissed with a wave of his hand.

Her head shake was immediate. Impressive, even, considering most of his employees had all but cowered even as they stared at him with wide, marvelling expressions.

Was he a man who was feared?

Something suspiciously distasteful soured his mouth. But he dismissed it in the next breath. No point inventing unsavouriness where there might be none.

What was more interesting was the way Imogen's gaze rushed over him, as if she was confirming for herself that he was indeed in shape, at least outwardly, before she responded. 'Be that as it may, I'm sure you'll agree it's prudent to get a doctor's opinion…' She paused. 'Unless you did that already. On the island?'

He frowned, then shook his head. 'Petros and Yiayia—the old woman—saw to my recovery in the weeks after they took me in,' he said.

'So a doctor didn't officially check you out? Weren't you curious to rediscover who you were?'

He almost smiled at the hint of disapproval and bewilderment in her voice. But her eyes were roving over him again—did she even know she was doing it?—and that charge he'd experienced when he'd taken her hand and helped her off the boat returned, stronger. More visceral. Awakening senses he hadn't even thought about, they'd been so surprisingly dormant.

But if he was to take back control of his life—
and didn't it feel as if he'd been holding his breath
to do just that ever since he opened his eyes to
feel Petros hauling him out of the grasp of a wa-
tery death?—he needed to control the demands
of his raging libido.

For now.

'Just because you stormed into a sleepy village
to stake your claim on me doesn't mean everything and everyone there was backward.'

Her eyes darkened with a flash of affront. 'I
didn't mean—'

'But I do take your point. The medical attention
I received when I was rescued was enough to put
me on the road to physical recovery. That took
the better part of four months.' Memory rushed
in, making his skin clammy and his gut tighten.
Those first days, when pain had been his con-
stant companion, and Petros's questions had only
drawn blanks, a part of him had offered to just…
be if he was spared death.

Should he have made a better bargain? Perhaps.

'As to my mental state…' He paused, unsure
why he was unwilling to mention the debilitat-
ing headaches that sprang up whenever he dug
too hard into his psyche. 'You are living proof
that things work out the way they're supposed to.'

Her eyes widened. 'So you were relying on
the…cosmos to work things out for you?'

He gave a low laugh, which also seemed to surprise her. 'You tell me, *matia mou*. Has biding my time in the past worked to my advantage or not?'

She blinked, then swallowed. Then her gaze dropped from his in a searing display of avoidance that gave him the answer he needed. 'I guess it has,' she murmured eventually.

'There you have it. I will see this doctor you wish me to. If that is what will please you?' he tossed in, just to witness what her reaction would be.

Heat flowed into her face and she licked her bottom lip again—a gesture that pinpointed her nervous state, while driving him quietly insane—and nodded. 'I do… I mean it will…for prudent reasons.'

He hid a grimace at that addendum. 'Then we'll get it organised in due course. But first…' He looked around, then back at her, his eyebrow raised.

She jerked forward, clearing her throat delicately. 'Yes. I'll show you around, then I'll let you rest while I get in touch with your doctor.' She paused a few feet from him and he realised that without her shoes she was petite, the top of her head barely coming up to his chest.

A small, delicious morsel.

He gritted his teeth against the heat that

pounded his groin and concentrated on the words she was speaking.

Yes, he was supposed to rest. When in fact relaxing in any way, shape or form was the last thing he wanted to do.

For the first time in his memory he felt alive. Truly alive. And with each breath he took, he felt the acute weight of everything he'd missed.

Still, he pursed his lips against protest and indicated she lead the way. From the flash in her eyes, Yiannis... Zeph was sure he'd riled her further.

And surprisingly...he wanted to keep doing it. Wanted to drag reaction out of her. Make colour continually stain her smooth cheeks. Make that bountiful chest rise and fall just so he could blatantly admire it.

Theós, he'd become an animal he didn't recognise somewhere between leaving Efemia and boarding the yacht.

Or had he always been like this with her?

All thoughts ceased when she pressed a button for a lift and they stepped into it. A delicate scent assailed his nostrils and he didn't hesitate to breathe it in. To infuse his senses with it. Hunger was clawing its way through his veins when the doors slid open and she hurried out, her own nostrils flaring delicately as if she'd been unable to help herself but to breathe him in too.

Forcing himself to concentrate, he dragged his

gaze from the bouncy pertness of her ass, still enshrouded in that peculiar green sequin, and glanced around the space he purportedly owned.

The muted shades of rich dark wood and gold trimming and cream tiles followed them everywhere. It pleased and soothed, the theme striking a note of satisfaction that compelled him to believe he'd chosen this decor himself. He must have if he'd named the yacht after his mother.

'My parents,' he asked abruptly, his senses skittering in a different, urgent direction, a part of him shamed that he hadn't thought to enquire until now. 'Are they alive?'

She stumbled, then froze. The eyes that darted to his held an even greater measure of apprehension.

Just what the hell was going on?

Before he could grit that question out, her eyes shadowed, then dropped to the floor. Even before she spoke his gut was clenched against what he suspected would be unwelcome news.

'I'm sorry. They're not. Your father died about twenty years ago and your mother not long after that.'

Shards of loss cut through him. He breathed through it, his senses suddenly frantic for more information. 'Any other relatives I should know about? Sisters? Brothers?' His gaze dropped to her belly and an astonishing spear of yearning dug deep into him. 'Do we have children, Imogen?'

Her green eyes shadowed in shock. She swallowed and again shook her head. 'No, we don't. And…you're an only child so no siblings. You have a few very distant relatives working for you at Diamandis but, from what I see, you're not close to any of them.'

Not close to his relatives.

No best friends or even close friends.

No parents.

The hollow in his gut expanded. Before he could come within a whisker of feeling sorry for himself, he suppressed the emotion. Just how he was adept at doing so, he refused to examine in that moment.

'So you're my only close attachment?'

Her eyes flew to his. Widened. As if it hadn't occurred to her. Then her head jerked forward, threatening once again to dislodge the bun at her nape. 'I guess so.'

As he absorbed the information, she grew restless again, her arm sweeping out to indicate the wide hallway behind her.

'Shall we?'

'One last question. How old am I?'

'Oh. Um…you're thirty-four. You turn thirty-five next month. On the tenth.'

He absorbed that for several seconds, nodded,

then approached where she stood. Unable to resist, he raised his hands, drew a caress down her cheek with his knuckle. 'And you, sweet wife?'

Her breath emerged shakily, gratifying him with the knowledge that he wasn't experiencing his urgent, emotional unbalancing alone. 'Me? I… I'm twenty-five. I'll be twenty-six this Christmas.'

'Twenty-five? And managing a global corporation on your own while chasing down your missing husband? Impressive.'

Again her eyes widened. And he could've sworn she was on the verge of blushing at his compliment when that wariness returned with a vengeance, snatching what felt like a prize right out of his grasp.

Disgruntlement settled deep within him when she stepped away, then pivoted her whole body from him. 'Thanks.'

The response was cool. Almost flippant. As if she refused to allow herself to accept it. He reflected on that as they toured a vessel he'd named after a mother he couldn't remember. As he was shown a level of wealth he knew most of the people he'd left behind on Efemia would give a limb to possess.

But what struck Zeph most as he grasped the burnished steel handles of his personal dressing room, in a stateroom fit for kings, and pulled a

partition open to observe row after row of dark
bespoke, impressive suits, priceless watches and
hand-stitched shoes, was the stark emptiness he
suspected wouldn't disappear even if his memories returned. Because it was an emptiness
shrouding that recurring dream every night since
his rescue.

That of a boy abandoned to loneliness, pain,
devastation. And fury. A lost boy seeking that
same *meaning* with a desperation that had Zeph
tearing awake with a thundering heart and an
empty soul.

Perhaps it was to deny those substantial emotions that he turned, reached out, and did what
he did.

Everything inside Imogen shrieked awake when
Zeph lowered his head and brushed his lips over
hers.

She gasped, her fingers rising to touch her lips
when he retreated almost immediately. 'Wh-what
was that for?'

He shrugged, a rich and fluent movement
that was mesmerising and arousing in equal and
shocking terms. 'An experiment. Seeing if I can
shake something loose.'

She took a step back. Then several. Pivoting,
she headed determinedly for the phone on the
bedside table.

'What are you doing?'

'Scheduling an appointment with your doctor like we discussed.'

Narrow-eyed displeasure feathered over his face. 'I didn't think it would be this soon.'

She paused. 'You don't want to be checked out immediately? You have amnesia!'

'And what is the doctor going to do exactly? Give me a pill that miraculously restores my memories?'

'I don't know. That's the whole point. We don't know what we're dealing with. Surely you'll want to know so you'll know how to start getting better?'

His head canted to one side, a gesture she remembered well. It was a pre-taunt tell. Which should've adequately warned her what was coming. It didn't. 'Are you that opposed to kissing your husband that you'll instigate medical intervention to avoid it?'

'I…what? That's absurd!' She shook her head, to get common sense reinstated and the memory of how sizzlingly good his lips had felt on hers out of her mind. 'This…your health should be our priority. Not…not…' She stopped, took a deep breath, then cringed when she realised she was blushing.

'Not discussing why my wife blushes crimson when I so much as look at her legs?' He shrugged.

'I'm intrigued by it all, truth be told. And I'd much rather delve into that than…' His long fingers gestured at his head and he grimaced in distaste and frustration.

Slowly, she returned the receiver to its cradle. If she didn't know better, she'd think Zeph didn't want to find out exactly what was wrong with him. Which was absurd. And puzzling.

The ruthless shipping magnate who'd delivered ultimatum after ultimatum, turning a chillingly blind eye to all her pleas for mercy, wouldn't have hesitated to get to the bottom of why he'd lost ten months of his life.

Ten months.

In which he'd been content to idle his life away on a fishing isle. Perhaps he truly didn't want to know. But…if he didn't, where did that leave her?

That softening feeling she'd had when he asked about his age and his parents and *their children* still lingered. While she'd cautioned herself then that it was dangerous to let it, she hadn't been able to help the swell of empathy. And then yearning. And that way lay her ruin, if she wasn't careful.

She couldn't flounder under his mercy for ever.

The three years they'd agreed to remain married was coming up in a little over a year. And come hell or high water, she would stick to her goals.

Pursing her lips, she snatched up the phone again.

CHAPTER THREE

FOR THE THREE hours her husband retreated to his stateroom, Immie remained on tenterhooks, her nerves stretching by the second. Questions and scenarios teemed and tumbled over in her mind.

He'd been without his memories for ten months. What if they never came back? What if it went beyond the three years she'd agreed to stay married to Zeph?

Was amnesia even curable? Or was it a throw of the dice as to what happened, when?

If he didn't regain his memories soon, would there come a time in the next fifteen months when she'd have to come clean, if only to detach herself from this enforced bond so she could carry on with her plans to take back full autonomy of Callahan Shipping—the company she'd devoted most of her adult life to before Zeph and her father had thrown a marriage of convenience in her way—and reclaim her own life? And if she so chose, would this altered, seemingly considerate, *smiling* Zeph Diamandis stand in her way?

Hadn't she suffered enough living under the thumbs of powerful men?

Now, watching him stride across the third and largest deck on the yacht towards her, she willed, futilely it turned out, her every nerve ending not to shiver to awareness at the sight of him.

Dear God, had he always been this visually compelling? Or was it the mystery of his disappearance adding to the reluctant allure?

The question disintegrated under the force of his stare as he looked first into her eyes, then down her body with his fierce gaze. Every inch of her body strained against…*something* in his proximity. Until she wanted to scream. To throw herself in the plunge pool in the middle of the deck just to cool off.

'*Kalispera, glikia mou,*' he drawled when he reached her.

Scrambling, she latched onto the first thing that came to mind. 'Um…hi. You didn't change.'

He still wore the shorts and T-shirt he'd arrived in. And his feet were…bare. For insanely long moments she stared at them, wondering if she'd had way too much sun. Because only some sort of altered state would account for why she found Zeph's bare feet sexy.

She snatched her rapt gaze away, only to follow the graceful masculine line of his shrug.

'Nothing in my wardrobe seems satisfactory.'

Now she was certain she was losing her mind. 'I'm sorry…what?'

He shrugged again, then dragged his fingers

through his hair, threatening to leave her mouth gaping with the intoxicating picture he made.

Dear God, what was happening to her? Was she truly falling into the cliché of 'needing to get laid' to diffuse this sudden rampant lust haze overtaking her? When her two previous relationships before she'd married Zeph had all but fizzled out before they'd barely begun, leading her to believe her sex drive might be dysfunctional at best or broken beyond repair at worst?

'There are two dozen shades of grey and black and navy in there. It doesn't please me,' he elaborated, thankfully shoving her back into the present, and the mundane discussion of clothing.

But it wasn't as mundane as she wished.

Because even this felt like a weird role reversal from when she'd stepped off the private jet Zeph had sent to Texas to bring her to Athens.

He'd taken one look at her and summoned a handful of haute couture designers to his luxury apartment. Within hours she'd been the unwilling new owner of the latest designs and the darling of several renowned fashion designers.

Since then, as per his instructions, her wardrobe was refreshed on a seasonal basis without fail, with new and upcoming designers desperate for her to be on their 'to-dress' list. That keen desire garnered loyalty. Enough for her to trust their discretion if she were to make a request now.

Not that she intended to announce Zeph's presence to any of them. She might still be relatively unknown, since she rarely socialised, but her name wielded enough power to ensure they remained extra discreet if they wanted her business.

'I can arrange for a new wardrobe to be brought to the apartment this afternoon, if you'd like?' she said, eager for this task to take her mind off… every electrifying thing about him.

He inclined his head in an almost regal fashion, absorbing far too much of her focus. *'Ne, efharisto,'* he said, then he frowned. 'The apartment?'

'Yes, the chopper is waiting to take us into Athens. Your doctor is meeting us there in an hour. It's all arranged.'

His jaw rippled with displeasure for a moment before he shrugged. 'Very well. You're in the driving seat, *gynaika mou.* For now.'

She told herself she wasn't pleased that he'd dropped the Miss Callahan. And yet, for the second time since he stepped on the deck, addressing her with an endearment sent a fizzy spiral of… something through her.

'Do you want anything else before we leave?'

'Appreciated though it is, I'm beginning to feel like fragile glass. Enough with the fussing, Imogen. Let's get this over with.'

A quick text to her stylist to get the wardrobe

organised and she was grabbing her bag. Then she started when he reached for her elbow.

Either he didn't see her startled expression or he chose to ignore it as he led her into the lift and up the three decks to the top where the sleek chopper waited.

Like the other members of the crew, the chopper pilot's eyes were agog when he spotted Zeph. They exchanged words in Greek, with the pilot's face wreathed in smiles.

And through it all, Zeph kept a hold of her, his fingers meshed with hers.

And with each second her breath grew shallower, this unique sensation of holding her husband's hand throwing her for a loop. Which was why she mentioned it as soon as they were on board and the aircraft was winging its way north towards the Greek capital.

'You don't have to do this, you know?' she blurted before she could stop herself.

His eyes narrowed. 'Do what, exactly?'

'This.' She indicated the grip he had on her hand.

'And why not?'

'You'll soon find out so I don't think it's a big deal to tell you. You're a powerful man. You have a multibillion-euro business. You have homes around the world. You've dated some of the world's most beautiful women. But this…isn't like you. You're not prone to public displays. So you don't need to…keep holding my hand. Or whatever.'

His eyes glinted and even before he spoke her skin was tingling, her belly flipping over with nervous energy at the brooding expression filling his features.

'I see only one beautiful woman in front of me, *eros mou*. One who is wearing my ring and carrying my name. I am confident there is a cogent reason for making that choice, and that reason is not a titivating mystery as your tone implies.'

Not ready for the twist in conversation, she blurted out unguardedly, 'What do you want me to tell you? That we fell in love at first sight?'

His nostrils flared and that glint turned almost brooding, almost contemplative before he shook his head. 'At first sight? Perhaps not. But I'm willing to bet a few substantial assets that it was lust at first sight.'

She couldn't help the gasp that erupted from between her lips. She tried to hide it with a scoff. 'That is just your libido talking—'

'I most certainly hope so or I'd have to see the doctor for far more worrying reasons than the gaps in my memories,' he quipped briskly.

It took her a stunned moment to realise he was cracking a joke. A fraction more of that time for the laughter to spurt out of her. Then she was laughing hysterically.

And Zeph…

Something caught and tightened excitedly in her midriff as he too threw back his head and laughed. Free, unfettered humour, wrapping them in a cocoon so warm, so cosy, so thrilling, that her heart swelled with yearning.

An uncontrollable two minutes later, she realised the look on his face had changed, yet again. His gaze was sharper on her face, a fierce intensity that drilled into her as his scrutiny continued. 'You have an amazing laugh, Imogen,' he announced thickly.

Her own died away under the charges snapping between them. Charges that made her skin dance for entirely different reasons. Heat scorched between her legs, making her squirm in her seat.

He saw it, acknowledged it with a smugly masculine look as his gaze dropped to her chest. She didn't need to look down to know her nipples were at attention. She could feel them every time she took her suddenly erratic breaths.

'And you look even more spectacular when you're aroused.'

She shook her head, adamant not to let those seductive words seem beneath her guard. 'We're straying away from the subject.'

His lips quirked. 'Or I'd say we're exactly on point.'

And she was still mired in that state of stunned shock and awe when they landed on the rooftop of their exclusive apartment building near Kifisia in Athens. As with the crew on the yacht, she'd briefed the staff about their employer's return and requested discretion, so only the housekeeper and two butlers were waiting when Imogen and Zeph entered the stunningly appointed apartment.

Despina, the housekeeper in her sixties and one of the few women who'd known Zeph since birth, rushed forward, tears in her eyes.

A torrent of Greek was unleashed and, again, Imogen stood stunned when Zeph smiled and even allowed the older woman to kiss him on the cheeks. When she departed with an enthusiastic promise of his favourite refreshments, the older of the two butlers said quietly, 'The doctor has arrived, Kyrios Diamandis. He's waiting downstairs.'

Zeph nodded, his features settling into the kind of sharp focus she was used to seeing on the old Zeph. So much so, she felt a shiver rush through her.

Whether he sensed it or had actually seen her shiver, his gaze swung to her as they proceeded down several dove-grey-wallpapered hallways and into the vast living room decorated in tones of white and grey.

She watched him, breath held, as he looked around the room, then pinned his eyes on her.

'Something wrong?' he intoned, his deep voice rumbling through her.

'Just wondering if anything in here rings a bell?' she asked.

He looked around again, his hands popped in his pockets in that calmly assured way that left her stunned at the way he was taking all this.

'No, it doesn't,' he rasped finally. 'But that's not what's bothering you, is it?' he added.

Since she could hardly say that the brief glimpse of his old self had sent a frisson of alarm through her, she touched on one of the many subjects seeking dominance in her mind.

'As much as I trust the staff and employees, we won't be able to keep the news of your return under wraps for long. I give it a week at the very least.'

His lips thinned and midnight-blue eyes narrowed for a moment. 'I have a PR team, I suspect?'

'Of course.'

He nodded. 'Arrange a meeting with them. I'll let them know how I want this handled.'

She shouldn't have been surprised that, for a man who didn't know anything about his past,

Zeph was resuming the mantle of powerful magnate with such ease. She suspected he had been born with every imperious strain fully installed in his DNA.

So then who was the man who'd cracked jokes and laughed with her in the chopper? A long-buried and now resurfacing facet of Zeph Diamandis or a temporary aberration?

She tightened her gut against the very suggestion that she wanted it to be the former. She had no right to wish for anything where this man was concerned. What she needed to concentrate on was the future.

Her freedom. A release from this sterile marriage with her company fully under her control.

With that in mind, she tried not to react to the eyes pinned on her as she sent an email about the PR team meeting for later that afternoon.

Then she breathed a sigh of relief when Despina entered with two maids bearing trays of food.

'I'll go and get the doctor,' Imogen said hastily, ignoring the fact that she had staff to do that for her.

Zeph's steady, brooding gaze reverted to her as she went to take a step away from the charged atmosphere. But if she'd expected him to remain silent, she should've known better.

'You can run as much as you like. I'll always

catch you,' he said with deadly softness into the storm of electricity that was growing thicker in the room.

Immie stumbled.

Righted herself.

Took a deep breath.

All without looking back at him.

Because if that voice was any indication, she was terrified at what she'd see in his eyes. Hell, she was terrified anyway. Because this version of her husband seemed intently focused on what the previous version had coolly and effectively disregarded—any hint of an emotional connection between them.

And as she went to retrieve the doctor from the smaller living room, she promised herself she would conquer this new and unwanted hyper-awareness she'd developed around the husband who needed to, imperatively, remain at arm's length at all times.

Just how she would do that…she didn't know.

But she hadn't come this far, sacrificed this much, to fail within sight of her goal.

Determination reinstated, she showed the doctor into the living room.

She'd never met the older man before on account of Zeph being in rude health with a top-notch exercise regime in place the whole time she'd known him.

But now she watched the doctor's eyes widen as he took his patient in. Watched his professionalism slip a little as he shook hands with Zeph.

Just like with the yacht crew and the apartment staff, he started to speak in Greek, then switched to English in deference to Immie. 'It's… I am so incredibly pleased to see you alive and well, Kyrios Diamandis.'

Zeph nodded, and although his smile wasn't as wide, it was there nonetheless, fanning that flame inside Immie as she watched his sensual lips curve.

As she remembered his words to her minutes ago.

She pushed them away, concentrated on the exchange.

'As much as I'm happy to be seen, under these particular circumstances, I wish it wasn't necessary,' Zeph replied.

His eyes met hers as he said the words, and she bit her lip.

As much as she wanted to get on with her life, was she, somewhere deep down, a little relieved that they weren't locked in the perpetual state of rancour his craving for retribution had engendered?

Again, she pushed that thought away as the doctor nodded.

'*Ne*, I also. Let us attempt to get you back on

the road to recovery, *ne*?' he said, then glanced at Imogen. 'Your wife told me on the phone that she hasn't observed any outward signs of adverse health?'

Zeph's gaze lingered on her, staying for several seconds too long. 'She's correct. I feel fine.'

When the doctor nodded and beckoned his two assistants forward with cases that looked to contain medical equipment, Imogen took that as her cue to leave.

Zeph's voice stopped her before she'd made it three steps. 'Stay, Imogen.'

The command rumbled through her, delivering layers of electricity and indomitable power that rushed fever through her blood.

She told herself she was annoyed at the imperial demand, that he'd made it impossible for her to leave, given their audience. But when she returned to the seating area, and he snagged her hand before she could place distance between them, she knew she'd stayed because this new Zeph continued to compel her with effortless power.

It was a relief not to be the subject of chilling indifference or glacial fury.

She tried to brush away the keen awareness of his muscled thigh next to hers as the doctor glanced at her.

'If it's not too much trouble, tell me the circumstances of locating your husband, Kyria Diamandis. It might help with his treatment.'

Reminded of the incident—goodness, was it just this morning?—she paused to summon the right words.

Zeph's eyes glimmered at her, as if he found her hesitation amusing.

Imogen shrugged. 'It was no big deal, really. He was in church in a small Greek village with a bunch of the people I assume he's been living with since he went missing. He didn't know who I was when I said I was his wife but he eventually...gave me the benefit of doubt.'

If the doctor was hoping for a salacious tale, such as a confession that she'd blown in like a *telenovela* heroine just as her husband was about to marry another woman, she wasn't about to make his day.

Zephyr Diamandis might be one of the richest men in the world, but he'd guarded his privacy with jaw-dropping zeal, with his PR department working overtime to ensure the very same. Besides, the last thing she wanted was to be embroiled in a media circus.

The doctor nodded, and proceeded to examine Zeph. Who continued to eye her with open interest as if the doctor and his minions weren't present.

'Tell me what your last memory is before ten months ago, Kyrios Diamandis.'

Finally the amusement was wiped off his face. His lips pursed and the area around his mouth grooved. 'I'm sitting on a doorstep of a house. I can hear Greek voices around me so I'm assuming it's here in Greece, but I could be wrong. I remember I'm waiting for someone but I don't know who.' He shrugged but Immie suspected his thoughts weren't as carefree as he projected. 'I also have recurring dreams playing out exactly those scenes so it may be the memory originated from a dream instead of the other way around.'

The doctor nodded, glanced at his assistant who made notes on a tablet, unaware that Imogen was frozen into shocked stillness.

'Do you recognise the person you're waiting for when they arrive?' the doctor asked.

Zeph's lips thinned further, his jaw clenching tight before he answered. 'No. Because they never do.'

Her heart lurched and she bunched her hands in her lap to prevent them from visibly shaking. Sucking in a slow, even breath so his attention didn't stray to her, she swallowed.

But collecting her fraying composure didn't stop the snarled words she remembered starkly from flashing through her mind.

Because of your family's greed I lost my

grandfather and then my father. I sat on my doorstep in the rain waiting for a father who never came home again. Be thankful I only want marriage to secure this deal, and not a biblical eye for an eye, Miss Callahan.

Her heart twisted further when Zeph raised a hand to rub his temple. It was the first adverse sign she'd witnessed of his condition and her heart lurched for different reasons.

'It's imperative that you don't try to force the memories,' the doctor admonished gently, peering over his bifocals at Zeph and the hand worrying his temple, then her. 'If that memory brings on headaches, you should refrain from probing it too much. That goes for you too, Kyria Diamandis. Attempting to prod his memories could do more damage that way.'

As much as she wanted to feel relief for being let off the confessional hook, she also dreaded the weight of the secrets she needed to carry.

'So you're saying there's nothing at all that can be done?' Zeph asked.

Imogen tensed further, conflicting emotions and hope and faint alarm swirling through her. She definitely wanted Zeph to get better. But it struck her acutely she didn't want to deal with the old version of her husband. Not because she couldn't—because somehow being forced to face down the board members and keeping a multibillion-euro conglomerate afloat had uncovered a spine of steel she was extremely proud of—but because she simply…didn't want to. *Yet.*

And perhaps even for his own sake, she wanted this formidable but less…intense Zeph to stay awhile. She grimaced at the faint guilt that brought, pushed the whole notion away and focused on the doctor.

Who looked apologetic. 'Retrograde amnesia—which I'm fairly certain is what you have—resolves itself in its own time. You've lived with it for almost a year. How long it lasts is anyone's guess.'

'One day at a time is all well and good, but I have several months' worth of questions. There are some things I will insist on knowing, Doctor, whether they incite a headache or not. I should warn you about that now.' The words were soft but the intent behind them were implacable. And again, he said them with his eyes fixed on her.

The expression in the doctor's eyes said he knew he wouldn't be moved on that point. 'Then I suggest that it's done carefully, with a minimum of stress. The good thing is that you're back among the familiar with people who've known you some or all your life. That in itself is a great start.'

Zeph gave a low laugh. 'Minimum stress,' he echoed. 'That might be easier said than done.'

'Then I must insist on frequent monitoring. Perhaps once a week.'

Imogen nodded, eager to dispel that faint alarm she'd experienced. 'We'll be here so we can arrange for you—'

'No, we won't,' Zeph slid in smoothly but firmly.

Her eyes widened as she stared at him. 'Why not?'

He shrugged, then cast a look around the living room. 'I like it on the boat. We seem to have everything we need on board. For now, I'd like to make that my primary residence.'

'But… I need to be in Athens. I have work to do and I can't just abandon it to go live on the yacht.'

'From what I've seen everything you need to work is on board. We'll continue to do that. What isn't available will be organised, I'm certain.'

She wanted to snap that he couldn't just turn up and start ordering her life. But that would be a lie. She had stepped into his shoes because her new surname dictated she step up. She still had a responsibility to see it through. If nothing else, for the sake of expediting the one thing she craved above all else. The freedom she'd attain in a little over a year.

As her protest died on her lips, the doctor nodded in agreement. 'If that's where Kyrios Diamandis feels most comfortable then I recommend you heed it.'

Immie stopped herself from rolling her eyes, but not so much attempting to halt the flared panic and fizz of…something that broke beneath her skin.

While the yacht was a sprawling vessel with plenty of room, she couldn't help but feel as if she'd been…trapped.

In Athens, she had the safety of her office or the separate apartment she'd had to herself within Zeph's luxury penthouse. There, they'd lived separate lives, rarely seeing each other unless some social function or other dictated their joint attendance. Beyond that, she'd seldom interacted with Zeph.

Every week, he'd been away on some international business trip while she had been working furiously to get Callahan Shipping back on firmer ground.

But it had been one of those necessary but rare social gatherings that had thrown them together on the yacht the weekend he went missing ten months ago.

'I think you were already doing so, weren't you, *kyria*?'

She blinked and focused on the doctor. 'Hmm?'

The older man smiled. 'I have heard it straight

from Zephyr in the past that the yacht is his preferred place to relax.'

Her eyes widened as Zeph's own eyebrows shot up. Apparently neither of them believed he'd divulged something so...mundane but personal to the good doctor.

'I told you that?' Zeph mused.

The doctor smiled wryly. 'I may have suggested that you slow down once or twice in the past during your biannual physical. And the impression I got from you was that the yacht was the most desirable form of relaxation.'

Zeph's quietly intense gaze swung back to her. 'Then it's decided.'

Imogen opened her mouth, but every argument that arose sounded like opposition against the very tool that might aid Zeph's healing. Besides, if there was one thing she remembered clearly from the two brief but searing meetings during which Zeph had laid out his plans for their convenient marriage, it was that in the eyes of the public they were to appear like any married couple, any hint of animosity a violation of their agreement.

Leaving her newly returned-from-the-dead husband to fend for himself on a yacht while she remained in Athens would seem callous and uncaring at best and intensely cold-hearted at worst.

Beyond that she needed to remember that one

day, sooner or later, Zeph would regain his memories. And while she would fight to retain the independence she'd gained in his absence, she didn't want to place herself in his worse books by denying him what he wanted now.

So she cleared her throat. 'I'll need to put a few things in place but…yes, if that's what's needed, then we will return to the yacht.'

She tried to ignore the blaze of triumph in his eyes and the unnerving sensation that she'd set herself on a risky path whose destination she couldn't quite see. Fixing her eyes on the doctor, she cleared her throat. 'Is there anything else I… need to know?'

The doctor shook his head. 'Nothing else. I will stress, though, that this is a waiting game, so patience is very much imperative.'

She didn't realise she was knotting her fingers harder until she saw Zeph's gaze drop to take in the action.

'I think my wife wants me back. Very much,' he drawled, speculative heat in his gaze.

And while the words weren't suggestive in any way, she couldn't help the cascade of heat pelting over her body. Or the accelerated beat of her heart. She shook her head to dispel the sensations. 'You're alive and well. That's all that matters right now.'

The doctor nodded approvingly, even as Zeph's gaze mocked her. 'Is it?'

She cursed herself for the heat that lit her face. For the disturbing emotions that lurked beneath her skin, ready to explode at the merest instigation.

What on earth was happening here?

She kept her gaze pinned on the doctor, breathing in relief when he answered. 'I'll get some blood tests done but, for now, there's nothing more to do but monitor the situation.'

Immie rose to her feet and brushed clammy hands down her thighs. Without glancing Zeph's way, she summoned a smile. 'I'll leave you to it, then. I have a few phone calls to make before we leave.'

She turned and walked away, then her breath caught when she stepped into the hallway and realised Zeph was behind her.

Startled, she glanced into his narrowed, still faintly mocking eyes.

'A kiss before you go?'

She barely managed to catch herself before her jaw fell to the floor.

It was framed like a question, but the gleam in his eyes said it was something more. Perhaps even a foray into the heart of their relationship.

A part of her sagged in relief that she hadn't fallen over, because, of course, that would've definitively given the game away. Even if this game seemed to have suddenly developed higher stakes.

Looking into his eyes as she scrambled for ways to refuse—and disarmingly failing—she wondered if somehow Zeph knew the rules more than he was letting on. That his instincts weren't prodding him to toy with her. To what end?

To make her suffer more than she already had?

The slide of his thumb over her knuckles seemed both attention-claiming and an insistence.

Give me what I want...

His gaze compelled. And with each second she hesitated, she knew she was drawing more un-wanted speculation from Zeph.

So...stomach churning and with the certainty that she was about to take the first shaky step on this risky path, Immie leaned towards him and brushed her lips over his.

Except a *brush* was far from what happened next.

Before she could pull away, Zeph's hand was gliding up her throat and around to cup her nape, his fingers holding her firmly in place as he deep-ened the kiss. Brushing became sealing, and then his tongue was sweeping over the seam of her lips, tasting her with bold strokes that immedi-ately resonated between her legs. Her gasp was swallowed beneath the force of his exploration, the rough sound he made further causing those tiny explosions between her legs to intensify.

Imogen's brain was still in free fall when he released her. When those eyes raked her face and returned to linger on her tingling lips. Lips she realised she was licking a second later and immediately stopped.

But his taste was in her mouth, in her bloodstream. Suffusing her senses.

And...*oh, God*...she wanted more.

That traitorous thought sent her stumbling back, her breathing nowhere near normal as she dropped her gaze from his, in case he witnessed her flustered yearning, and hurried away to the sound of his very masculine drawl.

'Hurry back, *glikia mou.*'

He *was* toying with her, she assured herself as she went through their connecting apartments to the study she used when she worked from home.

Settling onto the seat behind her desk, she took another deep breath to calm her roiling emotions, then immediately reversed any gains by touching her lips.

God. That kiss.

No, she wasn't going to think about it. Whatever Zeph might be going through now with his memory loss, he was still the same man underneath. Hell, she'd even spotted a few of the traits she remembered, especially in that intense stare he kept levelling at her.

It was only because they'd spent just a handful of occasions—albeit emotionally fraught, for her—of extended time in each other's company that she was unnerved.

Sooner or later, he would grow bored. And his memories would return.

Then she would finally be free.

But what if they didn't?

She gulped down her apprehension and reached for her phone.

A ten-minute conversation with her PA and everything she needed to work from the yacht had been actioned. Immie bit back a sigh at how ridiculously easy it was to uproot her life in favour of a situation she could feel in her bones would be more turbulent than she wished.

Distracted, she wasn't aware she'd activated the video function on the next call until a face popped up on her screen.

'Oh, hey there. I was about to email you,' Noah Emery said.

Immie's smile was easier and open now.

Her deputy at Callahan had been invaluable these past ten months and continued to be.

An American like her, with college-quarterback good looks to match. She'd managed to poach him from a rival company when it'd become clear that her workload in managing Callahan Shipping while being an active member of the board of Diamandis would be nigh on impossible without further assistance.

'I've saved you the trouble, then.'

He smiled and nodded, his sandy hair immaculately styled and in place.

Not like Zeph's long, sexily tousled locks.

She stumbled back from that thought, a little alarmed at how it'd slipped so easily beneath her guard.

'I wanted to congratulate you on the Canadian deal. I saw the memo you sent to our lawyers this morning.'

Her smile widened further. 'Thanks. Here's to hoping they don't throw any more roadblocks in our way before it's done and dusted.'

'Yeah. But while we wait for that to go through, I was hoping to discuss some Callahan business with you. Are you free for lunch today? Your PA said you were at the apartment. I could grab something and come to you if you're working from home?'

She opened her mouth to answer just as Zeph appeared in the doorway.

He didn't enter. Just draped himself against the doorjamb, four fingers in each pocket in a picture of casual sexiness that made her throat dry.

And the way he watched her. As if she was

the most absorbing thing for miles. As if she was his personal project he intended to keep a keen eye on.

That singular, intense focus snatched all of her breath. She didn't need to scour her memories to know she'd never experienced anything like it. At every stage in her life, she'd fought to be seen. To be heard. More often than not with little success.

When she'd first discovered that her father had expected her to come into the world as a fully fledged male Callahan—via a tipsy conversation to his guests after an all-male hunting weekend in Texas when her father had believed she'd gone to bed—she'd been stunned, then hurt. Then she'd spent months being bewildered and indignant at the injustice of it. At the very unfair supposition when biology dictated that it was a purely fifty-fifty chance she would be born female.

It turned out biology didn't matter. Her father had willed it and expected it to happen. And when it hadn't, he'd laid the blame entirely at her feet.

Not once had he shifted his stance.

So yes, Immie knew what it was like to be overlooked, to be dismissed as a disappointment, to be isolated and ignored, and then sacrificed like a worthless pawn when the situation suited.

'Immie?'

She dragged her gaze from the man lounging in the doorway to her study and back to the screen. 'Um… I can't today,' she answered Noah. 'I have a full schedule.'

'Oh. Okay. Tomorrow, then? There's a new chef at The Hydra. I know you like their food.'

Aware of the eyes boring into her from several feet away, she cleared her throat. 'I'm going to be working remotely for a while, Noah. Just email or call with whatever you need me for until further notice.'

He frowned, light brown eyes filling with worry. 'Is everything okay?'

Zeph slowly straightened, that languidness disappearing as he sauntered into the room. And with each step, he took another large chunk of her concentration while making her intensely aware of his magnetic presence. 'Everything is fine,' she said with a forced smile. 'I'll be in touch when I've looked through the emails.'

He looked as if he wanted to push for more, but, feeling a little guilty, she ended the call.

Silence throbbed in the room.

When it got too much, she lifted her head and met his gaze head-on.

'Another demanding client?' he enquired, a bite in his voice.

She shook her head. 'Noah isn't a client. He's a colleague at Callahan Shipping.'

Midnight-blue eyes narrowed into serious slits. 'A colleague who invites himself over to lunch as and when he pleases?' That edge had intensified, even though his body remained relaxed. Deceptively languid.

'I work long hours most days. I've learned to be flexible with my working hours.'

'And he's been here to the apartment from the sounds of it. How accommodating of you.'

'He's an invaluable asset.'

That mocking eyebrow went up. 'Is he? Enlighten me how,' he invited bitingly as he reached her desk, and promptly perched on one corner.

Immie struggled not to glance down at his muscled thigh so close she could reach out and touch it. Touch *him*.

'Why do you want to know?'

His lips twitched but the humour from before was absent now. 'I didn't spend all three hours "resting" this morning. After almost a year of dealing with a blank space, I'm sure you'll understand how curiosity is difficult to resist. I have the broad strokes of my life. So if this Noah works for Callahan Shipping, which is a semi-independent company I happen to own, then he's technically my employee. So answer the question, Imogen.'

She swallowed, an abstract part of her wondering why the hell she was so on edge. 'He has a brilliant business mind. I was lucky he was willing to relocate from the States to Athens to help me run the company.' When he continued to level a stare at her, she added, 'He went to Harvard, graduated at the top of his class at Harvard Business School.'

When that didn't elicit more than an intensely bored expression, she bit her lip. 'You do know what Harvard is, don't you?'

One corner of his mouth quirked. 'Surprisingly, yes.'

'Then…?'

'You want to know why your little puppy's credentials don't impress me?'

Unlike her other emotions, she let him see her irritation. 'He's not my little puppy.'

'No? Sycophancy isn't undetectable with memory loss, you know,' he said. And while his tone was dryly amused, there was an edge to it.

Much as there'd been on the yacht when he'd talked about her trip to the nightclub.

Why that sent another fizz of electricity through her system, Immie was absolutely not going to accommodate. 'I don't know what you're talking about.'

His lips thinned for several seconds before he rose to his feet. 'The pilot is waiting. It's time to go.'

She opened her mouth to put forth a myriad objections. But when her gaze, which seemed incapable of not running over him, tracked him from head to toe, the words that emerged mildly stunned her. 'You want to leave already?'

Zeph's eyes glittered at her. 'I see no reason to remain here.'

'But…the things I ordered for you are on their way. You don't want to change?'

'You object to what I'm wearing?'

'Yes… I mean, no, but…' Her treacherous gaze tracked him again. 'It's just I thought you'd have found something here in the meantime.'

'I didn't. But I made a curious discovery though,' he mused.

Her skin jumped as he watched her with those brooding eyes. 'What?' she asked tentatively.

'I got an initial impression from the tour on the yacht. And it seems I'm gathering a distinct picture that we don't sleep in the same room. Or even share the same apartment. Why is that, *matia mou*?' he murmured. But it was a deadly sound that raised every hair on her nape. Reminding her—as if she needed it—that this man in front of her was just a different facet of the Zeph she knew.

She licked her lower lip, a motion that seemed to make his midnight eyes gain even more depth and mystery. Hesitation would be deemed evasion. She knew that.

So she scrambled to deliver a true but partial version of their circumstance. 'It was your idea.

You travelled a lot for business. And you were used to having your space, and this apartment was available. We didn't see a need to change the status quo where it didn't need to be changed.'

A flash of something she would've termed displeasure in anyone else's eyes came and went just as quickly. 'How long had we been married before we were parted?'

We were parted.

As if theirs had been an emotionally charged and heartbreaking severance instead of the cold, shocking mystery his disappearance had truly been. A disappearance that had come within a whisker of turning suspicious eyes on her until the authorities ruled her innocent. 'A little over a year.'

This time the emotion lingered a fraction longer in the nostrils that flared. 'So I left a relatively new bride behind?'

Why on earth did the murmured words send a heated blush flowing into her cheeks? She was the daughter of a brash and brazen Texan who'd had a dim view of the female of the species to the point of pretending they didn't exist until needed. Which meant that she'd been familiar with cuss words long before she'd shed her braces.

Imogen was silently repeating one of those unladylike cuss words when he spoke again.

'I have a lot to make up for and catch up with, then, in that case.'

'I…what? No, you don't,' she said, a little too hurriedly. Because her blaring instinct warned she didn't want to know what that meant.

He slowly prowled towards her as he spoke, causing her to retreat. Until the desk blocked her. She was clinging to the edge when he smiled down at her.

'I believe I do. I can't wait to begin. Did we have a honeymoon?'

'I…no.'

'Just as I thought. Then I can't think of a better place to start than with the honeymoon we didn't have.'

CHAPTER FOUR

VERY EARLY IN the mysterious journey that was his new reality, Zeph had decided to trust his gut instinct. Sure, he relied on his other senses when needed. His reasoning, observation and strategy had turned Petros's mediocre fishing business from a two-vessel, barely ticking over concern into a ten-vessel growing business in a matter of months. A factor he knew deep down had played into the older man's desire to keep him around, perhaps even pushing his daughter into a commitment she hadn't been totally ready for.

It was why he didn't need his gut to tell him Imogen wasn't being entirely truthful about their sleeping arrangements. Perhaps even keys areas of their married life.

But it was that pure gut instinct that had prodded him just now.

It was partly why he'd delivered that statement about a honeymoon he hadn't even thought of before it came spilling out. But once uttered, there was no taking it back.

And his wife's quickly masked shock only deepened the need to get to the bottom of the mystery surrounding his marriage, doctor's advice be damned. He might not know himself through and through, but he knew enough to know he wasn't a man who sat around and waited for things to go his way or for opportunities to fall into his lap.

For a moment the searing reminder that he had no immediate family to provide insight pained him. Had he inherited that characteristic from his mother or father? Perhaps even a loving grandfather or uncle?

Accepting the futility of such thoughts, he pushed the sensation away. The same way he'd been pushing away the urge to go digging for answers. After all, if his parents were dead and he had no close relatives to paint a picture for him, wasn't he just as lost now as he had been twenty-four hours ago?

He would tackle one problem at a time.

For now, his instincts insisted the one in front of him held supremacy.

Watching Imogen cycle through a myriad emotions, he decided to go one better. Up the stakes to unravel whatever this conundrum was. 'Or you can come clean with everything.'

'E-everything?' she echoed, then frowned as if hating herself for the shakiness in her voice. He'd seen echoes of that self-disgruntlement. As if even a hint of a flaw was anathema to her.

He shrugged inwardly. He didn't need instinct or the influx of memories to tell him he was the same. Perhaps that was part of the attraction between them?

'I'm not sure I know what you mean.'

'No?'

She shook her head, and he silently willed that knot at the back of her head to unravel. The acute need to sink his fingers into those lustrous locks mildly alarmed him. As had that pounding need he'd been restraining himself from acting on again since she'd left him with the doctor. Hell, he'd barely been able to pull back from that kiss.

So why resist?

She was his wife, after all, wasn't she?

He wasn't sure why he was holding back. Perhaps he was savouring what was to come. Had he been this patient before? Or was it something else? Something less…palatable?

He'd returned—by all accounts from the dead—and she'd barely even touched him. That flash of jealousy she'd exhibited in the church when she'd believed he was marrying another woman—which he admitted now had stoked something primal and possessive to life within him—was now carefully but firmly under control. Which was all the more dissatisfying in light of his own emotions when he'd heard that young buck attempting to inveigle his way into a private lunch with Imogen.

His *wife*.

Zeph couldn't deny there was distance between them. He might not remember every relationship he'd had in the past but even he knew a contented married couple didn't live in separate apartments. Or have separate sleeping staterooms on a private yacht.

He watched her open her mouth, no doubt about to issue another prim denial. An excuse. A less welcome alternative.

And he felt that primitive urge swell higher. 'I haven't gone down the unsavoury path of looking myself up online yet but I've learned enough about my business practices to know I'm not averse to tough negotiating. Is that what is needed now, *matia mou*? Or will my wife come willingly?'

He tried to ignore the fact that she seemed to wince imperceptibly every time he reminded her that they were married.

No matter. They had time. Time to delve into the mystery of why this woman, who awoke intrigue and carnal desire he hadn't experienced for any of the women who'd crossed his path in the last ten months, alternately looked at him with defiance and wariness.

He frowned inwardly. He hadn't…hurt her, had he?

His jaw clenched, willing her to give a positive answer so the unnerving sensation crawling through his belly would cease.

'I've already said I'll come and stay on the yacht with you,' she murmured, but that mildly bewildered look in her eyes didn't dissipate.

And that only made the churning in his gut intensify. He quelled it and nodded, telling himself to tread carefully. 'Good—'

'But a honeymoon isn't necessary,' she blurted. 'We've been married for over a year.'

'Barely enough time to feel like a boring old married couple. Were we estranged, Imogen?' he asked, boldly taking a chunk out of the mystery.

'No, we weren't,' she murmured after one too many beats.

He sidestepped the relief that oozed through him. 'Good,' he repeated, then held out his hand. 'We will buck a trend and celebrate our second wedding anniversary and our honeymoon in one go. So shall we?'

He gritted his teeth as she eyed his hand as if it were a coiled snake about to strike. *Patience.* His senses shrieked that was what was required here.

After an eternity, she crossed the room and placed her hand in his.

And that sonic explosion came again, rocking him on his feet.

He'd dismissed it as his over-exuberant imagination the first time it'd happened. Just as he'd downplayed the effect of that kiss and the way it'd thrilled his blood and roused his male senses.

Now he knew it wasn't.

His libido was alive and well, and eager for this intriguing woman who'd somehow taken his name but didn't act one little bit like a wife happy to be reunited with her husband.

And perhaps that was a tool rather than an obstacle. Or, at the very least, a satisfactory way to pass the time while he waited for his memories to return. He shrugged inwardly. At this point he was beginning to accept that nothing was off the table.

And if he had to seduce his wife in order to unravel this mysterious part of his life…well then, so be it.

What on earth was she thinking, agreeing to a honeymoon with Zeph?

What did that even entail?

Well, for starters, it seemed he wasn't willing to let go of her hand. Every subtle effort to withdraw it had been thwarted all the way through saying goodbye to the household staff, including a tearful Despina, and reboarding the helicopter.

This new state of play also, it seemed, included staring broodingly at her as they were transported back to the yacht. Thankfully, she managed to extricate herself from his sizzling grasp and take a full breath for the first time once she alighted.

Then she threw herself into busy mode. Her

fingers flew over her phone as she read and replied to emails and text messages.

Sensing his gaze once more on her, she looked up to find him watching her.

'Do you want something to eat? I'm sure something can be organised for you?' she asked, to hide the fluttering in her belly.

A smile cracked his lips. 'You seem determined to fatten me up. For what purpose? Do I need fattening up?'

'I... What?' Stumbling, she made the mistake of eyeing him from head to toe again. Which of course triggered that knowing smile that made her want to kick herself. 'No, of course not...unless you...' She shook her head. 'I know it's a Greek thing to always have refreshments available.'

'Indeed, but one still gets bored with an endless flow of *meze* after a while. Be assured that when I'm hungry, you'll be the first to know, *eros mou.*'

Her stomach jumped at the endearment. She'd been in Greece long enough to learn a few of them. *Eros mou* held much more earthy connotations.

Love. Lust. Intimacy.

Things a honeymooning husband in love wouldn't hesitate to shower his wife with. Her fingers curled over her phone as her body reacted to it. Skin grew hot and taut. Nipples hardened and strained against satin. And between her thighs… God, had she ever felt such urgent need?

While she'd found the man she'd married compelling, his chilling demeanour and indifference had restrained the unwanted bites of awareness she'd experienced at those first meetings. And even when she'd unwillingly accepted how handsome and utterly captivating Zeph Diamandis was, she'd managed to curb any wayward yearning before it'd developed into something neither of them wanted.

This new version of Zeph…mesmerised her. He made her *burn* with awareness. His proximity wrecked easy havoc on her senses while her heart raced with…hunger.

She tried to breathe calmly through it, to not show in any way how *affected* she was.

Because it seemed Zeph was determined to wring reaction after reaction from her. And she couldn't let that happen.

She pounced on her phone when it pinged with a message, then breathed a sigh of relief when she read it. 'The stylists are on their way. They should be here in about fifteen minutes.'

His lips twitched with a touch of mild disinterest, then he draped one muscled arm over the back of his seat. 'Fifteen minutes gives us enough time.'

Her senses jumped and scrambled helter-skelter once more. 'Time for what?' she all but screeched.

His amusement intensified. 'Time to tell me more about the intricacies of my company,' he replied coolly.

Oh. She swallowed. Not what she'd expected. But she still needed to be delicate. 'What do you want to know?'

'Let's start with structure. Then you can tell me how Callahan Shipping—which I'm assuming is your family company?—came to be involved.'

Choosing her words carefully, she gave a PR version of what she knew about his company. Then took a breath and added, 'There was a threat of Callahan Shipping being disposed of in the deal you made with Avalon.'

'Unless it was on the verge of bankruptcy or woefully mismanaged, you could've walked away with something, no?'

She shook her head. 'It wasn't as big as Diamandis obviously, but I didn't want that.'

'Why not?'

Old feelings of inadequacy and bitterness rumbled through her, wounds she'd never quite been able to fully heal. But she had spent a considerable part of her life suppressing it, it was fairly customary to slap more bandages over it, numb it beneath layers of suppressed emotion. So she could focus on answering him again without arousing the sharp spikes of his suspicion the way she'd come close to doing. And the best way she knew how to achieve that was to concentrate on herself.

On the parts Zeph didn't know about her. And if that made her pathetic in his eyes… She shrugged mentally and ploughed on.

'I spent my whole life trying to prove to my father that I was as capable as the son he never had. I wasn't about to step aside and let everything I'd worked for be tossed away.'

Another gleam in his eyes, perhaps even a hint of that pride she'd spotted earlier lit through the midnight-blue depths. Sparking something far too close to pleasure inside her. 'So you fought for what you wanted.'

'Yes.'

'And you got it?'

She nodded. 'Eventually, yes.'

'I'm glad.'

Are you?

She exhaled in relief when the question didn't slip free.

'You look sceptical,' he observed, right on cue. 'You doubt my sentiment?'

'We're both attempting to navigate this new normal, Z-Zeph. If I seem…surprised about things, that's the reason why. We don't need to dissect everything—'

Despite his relaxed stance, she could feel the rumbles of his aura, the sheer magnetism she suspected would overwhelm even when he slept. 'Say that again,' he invited thickly, his gaze raking her face.

'What?'

'My name.'

She slicked her tongue over her dry lips. 'Why?'

Those midnight-blue eyes were almost black now, his gaze shamelessly fixed on her mouth. 'Because I find that I like hearing you say it.'

She shook her head to deny that and to dispel the foolish sorcery he evoked with each word. 'There's nothing special in the way I say it.'

'I beg to differ,' he drawled, a thickness in his tone that escalated that spark into flames. Flames that shamelessly flared all over her body igniting illicit lust in their wake. 'Say it, Imogen,' he commanded, his tone low, deep and utterly mesmerising.

'Zeph,' she whispered.

He surged forward, his movements almost involuntary as he ran his thumb over her lower lip. Calluses, probably from the taxing job of hauling nets from the ocean, grazed over her lips, sending further sparks through her. Lean cheeks shadowed by sculpted cheekbones made him stunningly handsome. But it was the air of confidence that clung to him that drew her. And she suspected most women to their doom.

'If your husband were to kiss you again, would you run away in terror the way you did last time?'

'I—I didn't run away.'

'Perhaps not physically. But I felt the distance. I want that distance gone, Imogen.' The growled determination behind that statement sent another wave of heat through her.

Oh, dear God...

She struggled to breathe as he continued to caress her lips, slowly, back and forth, his eyes following his movement with rabid focus. 'We shouldn't... You're not in a—'

'Cite my memory loss one more time and I'll shut you up with my tongue.'

Sparks that probably shouldn't have felt so damn thrilling lit her insides. 'Is that a threat?'

'Oh, no, *matia mou*. It's a very vigorous promise. One I can guarantee you will enjoy.'

For a blind moment, Immie felt searing jealousy.

For all the women he'd displayed such single-minded craving for in the hazy past. Perhaps even for the future lovers who would get to enjoy this rabid carnal attention from the most compelling man she'd ever encountered.

Then she was dragged back to the present by his insistent thumb, seeking entry between her lips. Lips that were parting almost of their own accord. Because the sorcery he was enacting was too hypnotic to resist.

But she had to.

She needed to remind herself that this wasn't the true Zephyr Diamandis. This was the imposter wearing his skin until his true self emerged once more. And as much as the sensation zipping through her bloodstream was seducing her to succumb to this…moment of sweet madness… she couldn't.

Because to do so would be to risk the very freedom that had fuelled her determination to find her lost husband. Freedom she could now pursue.

Because in a year, she would be free. She would've served her time.

The three years she'd agreed to would be up!

Divorced from Zeph Diamandis with the company she'd nurtured intact and her sacrifice behind her.

With that reminder in mind, she pulled away, ignoring the sharp pang of disappointment triggered by eluding his touch.

'Not citing doesn't mean any of this is still a good idea. Or what I want,' she tagged on in a bid to firm her resolve. So what if it came out weak and a little desperate?

What if it seemed to rouse something in his

eyes? Determination? A resolve much thicker and weightier than her own?

She swallowed the darts of alarm, and firmly grasped the tail-end of their previous discussion. 'Yes, so to answer your question, Callahan is mine but falls under Diamandis's overarching purview.'

For an age, he stared at her. Then he nodded. 'Tell me about the board members. Who impresses, who disappoints. Who will smile at me while stabbing me in the back.'

She couldn't quite hide her grimace, and her breath caught when one corner of his mouth quirked.

'That bad?'

Her shoulders sagged and she realised she'd been tense at the direction of his conversation where perhaps she needn't have been. 'Only if you consider a bunch of men alluding to a woman's place not being the boardroom or being CEO of a conglomerate on a far too regular basis a bad thing.'

His eyes glinted and she caught a glimpse of the formidable tycoon in that look. The one men who valued their skins bent over backwards not to invite. 'But you didn't let that cower you.'

She shrugged. 'I held my own. I'm used to doing that when it counts.'

Those eyes narrowed. 'Does that include with me?' he enquired silkily.

She shivered, then decided she had nothing

to lose by stating the truth. 'I won't let you run roughshod over me when it counts.'

'I'll consider myself duly warned.'

Imogen had a feeling she'd need to keep that statement alive and burning at the forefront of her mind since her emotions and body were behaving in ways she found disconcerting. Luckily, she was saved from further torment when the head steward approached to let them know the stylists had arrived.

She scrambled up, very much aware of his solid presence behind her as they descended one deck to the more intimate one where the designers waited.

Zeph barely glanced at them as they scurried about unzipping garment bags. She knew why when he immediately intercepted her when she tried to make a discreet exit.

She gulped when he loomed in front of her, one eyebrow slanted upward. 'You always seem in a hurry to leave my presence. A lesser man would have a complex about his wife fleeing his presence when they're supposed to be on their honeymoon.'

She didn't miss the fact that he exempted himself from that weaker man bracket. 'But…you don't need me to choose your attire for you,' she whispered heatedly.

'No, and yet I want you to stay. I would appreciate your input. And after all, you need to appreciate the view too.'

Her eyes widened even as colour swam into her cheeks. Her gaze darted to the stylist who had discreetly turned away. Zeph suppressed a smile and proceeded to tug his T-shirt over his head. His shorts were kicked away next and he stood in his boxers, tall, proud, blatantly near-naked and unselfconscious, with both hands propped on his lean hips.

Sweet heaven, he was breathtaking. Too much. Heat billowed between her thighs and she swallowed the moan that threatened to escape.

Desperately reaching for her phone, she started to glance down at it, hoping for some sort of electronic intervention. The device was plucked out of her hand a moment later and tossed onto a cushioned seat several feet away.

'Hey, you can't do that.'

His face hardened. 'I'm your boss. In that capacity you'll find I can do whatever I want.' He pointed to a seat. 'Sit.'

Oh, yes. The very much insufferable Zephyr Diamandis was alive and kicking in this version, too. But since he was indeed her boss, and she'd agreed to this…farce, she had no choice but to obey.

She sat down.

Then spent the next hour with her hands clenched tight in her lap, biting her tongue so it didn't hang out like a teenage groupie as her husband strutted around like a supermodel who'd stepped off the pages of *GQ* magazine.

With the early evening sun over the glittering Aegean as the perfect backdrop against the vibrant and bronzed breathtaking pillar of masculinity, each audacious exhibition made her belly flip over in saucy excitement, until she feared she would quietly hyperventilate and expire where she sat.

And when he casually dropped questions like, 'Do you like this?', 'Does this please you?' Imogen felt as though she were being treated to her own version of that erotic movie that had taken the world by storm a handful of years ago. Only with the shoe thrillingly on the other foot. And even if the power dynamic wasn't quite as favourable for her, there was enough of it for risqué and illicit fantasies to reel through her mind, sending arrows of lust and need between her thighs as she nodded or rejected at will.

She was partly regretful but mostly relieved when it was all over and the designers had taken their leave. Of course that didn't mean reprieve from Zeph.

Imogen turned from watching the departing stylists to find him frowning down at his left hand. The new lemon-coloured polo shirt and khaki cargo pants he'd kept on highlighted every inch of bronzed flesh on show, his tousled hair lending him a rakish look that continued to play havoc with her equilibrium.

But it was what he was doing—running his thumb over his ring finger specifically—that made her heart jump into her throat. She had an inkling of his thoughts, and yet she wasn't ready for the words that came out of his mouth.

'I wasn't wearing a wedding ring when I woke up. You didn't mention it when you listed what I was wearing the last time you saw me. Since you haven't enquired about it, I'm assuming there wasn't one in the first place?'

She shook her head. 'No, there wasn't.'

Rapier-sharp eyes cut into hers. 'Why not?'

She pursed her lips as her mind raced to find an adequate, non-harmful answer.

But…how long could she keep skirting this issue? Because it was clear he knew there was something missing besides just his memories.

'Tell me, Imogen,' he insisted, his voice thick with command.

Crossing her fingers that she wasn't making a mistake, she exhaled. 'You never gave me a reason why. You simply stated that you wouldn't be wearing one.'

His nostrils flared and he snagged her left wrist. Her fingers involuntarily curled around his when he raised her hand and stared at the wedding and engagement rings adorning her finger.

After an age, his thumb slid over the diamonds, just as intimately as he'd caressed his own skin. Heat unfurled through her belly, but alongside it came another sensation.

Anticipation? Hope? For what, exactly? She shook her head as the emotion persisted. As it thickened and attempted to find fertile soil to grow.

'Well, I've changed my mind,' he announced.

Why on earth did that send her heart thumping against her ribs? Whatever he did during this period while he waited for his memories to return, it didn't change the fact that they were still locked in a marriage of convenience. That she had no business letting this…intensely fascinating and compelling version of Zeph Diamandis slip beneath her guard.

'Are you going to give me the name of our jewellery broker or should I go rummaging?'

The very idea of Zephyr Diamandis rummaging for anything made her lips twitch. Which was, again, madness in itself. Hadn't she reassured herself that the time he'd cracked a joke, reminding her that he was the first to make her laugh harder than she had in as long as she could remember, was a one-time indulgence?

She jerked as his thumb swiped over her lips.

'I'm attempting not to be insulted that you keep drifting away from me mentally and physically.'

The possessive bite in his voice piled another truckload of coals onto the fire already smouldering inside her.

'I…yes, if that's what you want, I'll make it happen,' she said with a far too husky voice.

She told herself she strode away from him to return to her desk to call her PA simply to get some breathing room. But her voice—and her insides—didn't feel as firm as her assistant answered.

'*Kalismera*, Mrs Diamandis. Is everything okay?'

No, she wanted to blurt.

'Yes, thanks, everything's fine, Agatha.'

'How can I help, Mrs Diamandis?'

Aware of the gaze fixed on her, she gathered her tattered composure together and answered. 'I need you to have the Diamandis jewellery broker brought to the yacht tomo…' she paused as Zeph gave a firm shake of his head, then cleared her throat '…this evening.'

'Of course, Mrs Diamandis. Anything in particular you'd like to see?'

Immie bit the inside of her lip, attempting to channel her husband's immense authority for half a second, and failed. Throwing caution to the wind, she winged it. 'He'll know what we need. Contact the chopper pilot to arrange transport.'

'Yes, of course.'

She hung up to find Zeph watching her. 'What?'

'Watching you wield power is sexy,' he drawled, his arms reaching out.

She had time to step away. So why didn't she?

Why did she remain standing, her senses leaping and somersaulting as he tugged her close? As his hands slid over her waist and boldly cupped her behind?

As she felt her husband's hot, muscled body for the first time.

Not even at their wedding had he held her this close.

Because theirs had been a cold and short ceremony in a formidable building that had been Athens' equivalent of city hall, with only his lawyers acting as witnesses.

It'd been over in under half an hour, after which he'd deposited her at his Kifisia home and promptly returned to the office and she'd been introduced by his butler to her new, *separate* apartment.

Every single reason for that remained real and alive, if temporarily shrouded by Zeph's amnesia. And yet caution seemed to be just out of reach and temptation spiralling through her, urging her to wrap her arms around that trim waist, plaster herself closer to his sublime body.

She scrambled around for something to say to diffuse that treacherous feeling. 'Thank you.'

'No. *Efharisto*,' he murmured instead.

'What are you thanking me for?'

He shrugged, the movement sliding his torso against her front, turning the tips of her nipples diamond-hard. 'Among other things? Coming to find me,' he said.

There was no hint of humour in that statement, just a deeply solemn recognition in his hypnotic eyes. An unspoken acknowledgement of her actions.

'Ten months is a long time. Others would've given up. Why didn't you?' he prodded.

Because I needed to know, unequivocally, one way or another before I grasped my freedom.

She chose a less volatile but truthful response. 'Call it gut instinct. I needed proof, one way or another.'

Would he be this appreciative when the full truth came out? When he discovered that beneath all the reasons why she'd needed to find him was a fraction of selfishness for her own ends?

She swallowed and suppressed the pang that thought produced, instead reaching for the question that had been niggling at the back of her mind since this morning. 'For a man who couldn't remember his past, you seemed...accommodating of your situation. Did you…did you not want to know what happened to you?'

His eyes grew shadowed and for almost a minute she thought he wouldn't answer. 'My injuries weren't life-threatening when I was found but neither was I in a state to go on a hunting spree. I was repeatedly reminded how close I'd come to dying. I had no other medical facility to compare to the one on Efemia so I accepted my slow nursing back to health.'

She frowned. 'But…didn't Petros or any of your rescuers make any effort to get to the bottom of who you were?'

His lips pursed, then a wry smile curved his lips. 'I was reassured efforts were being made in the first few months. You were there. You saw how…laid-back they were. In hindsight I suspect there was no great desire for things to change once the initial efforts had come to nothing.'

'You mean Petros? He and his family wanted to keep you to themselves?' The words came out sharper than she'd intended and she couldn't deny that the possibility that she might not have found him, ever, struck her a little too raw for comfort.

He shrugged, but the fleeting tightening of his lips said he took that a little more seriously than he wanted to admit. 'Perhaps.'

Her shock grew. 'And you were happy with that? It doesn't—'

She stopped herself before she said something his brilliant mind cottoned onto. Something she wouldn't be able to take back.

'It doesn't seem like the man you know?' he finished.

Swallowing, she jerked out a nod. 'That man… he would've stopped at nothing to discover who he was. What he'd left behind.'

Zeph glanced around him, then at the stunning view beyond the deck, before his gaze returned to her. 'Maybe I always knew I would return. There seems an inevitability to all this.'

Her breath caught. 'There is?'

His mouth twitched. 'Don't look so distressed, *matia mou*. We have lost a little time. But I intend for us to more than make up for it.'

The words were too ominous to stop the shiver that raced through her. And this close, he felt it. His eyes narrowed and his arms tightened. Even more alarmed by how much she wanted to stay, to delve deeper into this fascinating aspect of Zeph, she cleared her throat and pushed away.

He resisted her for a fraction of a second before he set her free, the faint tic in his temple conveying that he wasn't too pleased about that.

Ignoring the thrill that sent through her blood, she went to retrieve her phone. 'I really need to catch up on work. Dinner is normally served at eight, unless you prefer it to be later?'

He waved her away, his eyes following her as she headed for the stairs. 'Eight is fine. And, Imogen?'

She looked over her shoulder, that jumpiness taking an even firmer hold on her. 'Yes?'

'There will be many more discussions in the coming days. I hope you're prepared for that.'

'I know.'

'*Kalos.*'

Good.

But would it be for her?

CHAPTER FIVE

I⊤ STRUCK IMOGEN as she prepared for dinner two short hours later that it hadn't even been twenty-four hours since she'd found Zeph.

It felt as if she'd lived a whole year and been on several emotional roller coasters since she'd stepped into that church. So she wasn't surprised when her hands trembled a little as she secured the gold hoops in her lobes. The turquoise and gold paisley bohemian sundress she'd chosen was light, flared and airy enough to swish about her mid-thigh as she examined herself in the mirror.

Dinner was being served on the aft deck on level three and she recalled the breeze was cooler there at night. Enough for her to leave her hair down after brushing. Spritzing her favourite perfume at her pulse points, she assured herself she wasn't nervous. That the butterflies cavorting giddily in her belly were to be expected.

A set of gold bangles and bone-coloured wedge shoes completed the outfit, then she had no more reason to linger.

Heading up from her stateroom, she furiously debated how to get through dinner with Zeph without falling under the magnetic spell he seemed to have cast around her.

Only to realise halfway through their first course that she might not need to go on the offensive.

The Zeph who'd arrived within a minute of her reaching the designated deck had been withdrawn, the lines around his mouth pinched. Even the gaze that had slanted over her, although missing nothing, had held a faint shadow of bleakness.

His voice had been a low, deep rumble as he'd greeted her and held out her chair.

Then he'd lapsed into brooding silence.

For alarming minutes, Imogen had wondered whether she was witnessing yet another facet of him. One she realised she didn't particularly know how to deal with. Not that she was particularly adept at handling the other two.

Then, as the staff approached with their after-dinner drinks, she realised what was happening when she caught his wince at the sharp footsteps.

'Are you feeling unwell?' She kept her voice soft and low.

He flicked her a hard little glance, his lips tightening a touch before he answered. 'Headache. I get them sometimes.'

That startling softening inside made her clench her gut. But like before, empathy slipped out before she could contain it. 'Did the doctor give you anything for it?'

'Nothing that has made a meaningful difference.'

His gaze rested on her for a few more seconds. 'Did I get them before?'

She shook her head. 'Not to my knowledge. You were always as healthy as a horse.'

His mouth twitched with wry amusement. 'Far better than feeling as if I've been kicked in the head by one.'

That softening arrived again, more insistent than before. She bit the inside of her cheek to stop herself from uttering the words that wanted to emerge. She couldn't do this. It made no sense for her to feel this way towards the man who was hell-bent on retribution against her and her family.

But that man didn't feel like the one sitting in front of her. The man who was clutching his espresso cup with white knuckles, stoically enduring the pain he was in.

'Can I help?' Something eased and settled inside her the moment she said those words.

He looked at her, his gaze resting on her face in that probing manner as if he was trying to decipher her thoughts. After an age, his lips twisted. 'Thank you, but there is nothing you can do that hasn't already been tried.'

Imogen swallowed her next retort. It was better this way, she told herself. Better to keep everything at arm's length the way it was before.

She glanced down at her half-eaten dessert, unwilling to consider where her appetite had suddenly fled. Why there was a faintly hollow space in her stomach. Surely she wasn't feeling dejected because he had rejected her offer of help?

Because that would mean…

No, she wasn't even going to consider that. Caring in any way for this man would only lead to a dangerous imbalance that would weaken her position in the end.

She started when he stood abruptly. 'Walk the deck with me,' he said.

She frowned. Opened her mouth and then shut it again. As much as she wanted this evening to be over so she could flee to the safety of her room, there was still the matter of the jeweller's visit.

She glanced at her watch, a little perturbed to see it was nearly ten p.m. 'Are you sure? It's been a long day for you. Look, I can push the jeweller's visit to tomorrow…?'

He was already shaking his head before she was halfway through her sentence, a determined set to his jaw that reminded her who she was dealing with. 'No. It's happening tonight.'

She frowned inwardly, wondering why this was so important to him. Then she gave up. From the moment she'd met him, she'd known that Zeph's mind was a labyrinth that would stump most normal human beings. 'We won't be any less married tomorrow without the ring, you know.'

Wry humour twisted his lips again despite the pain most likely throbbing at his temples. 'Who knows what will happen between now and tomorrow morning? I could tumble over the side again and go missing. At least when I wake up in a strange place again, I will know that I am a married man.'

She gave a small gasp. 'Is that why you're doing this? Because of some abstract identification purposes?'

For a long moment he remained silent, and then he shrugged. 'If I had known that I was married, perhaps it would've lent a little urgency to my decisions.'

Imogen was caught between feeling wavelets of desolation and a dash overwhelmed at the response. The thought of Zeph fighting his way back to her shouldn't have made her feel so elated. Because at the end of the day their marriage truly meant nothing emotionally. She would do well to remember that.

'Well, the chances of you going over the side of the boat twice feels a little remote to me.'

His gaze remained on her, probing again. 'Tell me about that night,' he said.

She shook her head. 'I don't think I'm really supposed to. The doctor said—'

'I don't care what the doctor said.' His face hardened, displeasure tautening his cheekbones. 'And I don't think leaving me in the dark is helpful to my state of mind.'

She swallowed. Hunted around but couldn't find anything to counter that argument. Averting her gaze from him to stare at the path of the moon over the glistening waters, she tried to gather her thoughts.

'You had just finished the Avalon deal. That is the big merger you had been working on for the better part of five years. To celebrate, you invited the CEO, Philip Avalon, and his family for a dinner party.' She let out a small laugh. 'The Avalon family is large. There were over fifty people on the boat that weekend, and I think at some point you were a little irritated by their exuberance. That last Sunday, they partied really hard. The crew said it was almost three a.m. before they eventually went to bed.'

Even without looking at him, she felt the power of his stare. 'And where were you?'

'I'd gone to bed about two hours before. You wanted to stay up and talk to Philip Avalon. The last time I saw you, you were on the upper deck. The head steward said he served you and Philip drinks at around one. Then Philip went to bed.

The security camera filmed you standing at the aft railing after that with a drink in your hand.'

His eyes narrowed. Then his lips thinned. 'Was I drunk?' The question was rasped, filled with surprising self-loathing.

'I don't think so. You were never a heavy drinker,' she found herself reassuring. 'I think you just joined Philip because he was known to indulge on occasions like that, just like the rest of his family, and you wanted to be an accommodating host.'

He nodded, the tension easing a touch from his shoulders. 'And then what happened?' he pressed in a tight voice.

'Then you fell over. We'd just left Santorini. Philip had expressed an interest in purchasing a private island so the captain was instructed to sail us and the Avalon family there by morning. No one knew where you were until the morning when we woke up.'

He remained silent, willing her to continue.

'There had been a light rain during the evening. Normally the crew are quite good at making sure everything was taken care of. But with their hands full with the party and taking care of the guests, the patch of rain left on the deck hadn't been cleaned up yet. You...stumbled a little as you turned away from the railing and you hit your head. We're not sure whether a strong wave rocked the yacht but the next moment, you went overboard. Anyway, I called the police, they reviewed the security footage and started a search.'

She took in a long breath, the memory of those first few weeks, the frantic search for one of the world's most powerful and influential men, and the sometimes thinly veiled suspicion aimed her way, all rushing to the fore once more. 'The authorities didn't have high hopes, even at the start. The current was quite fast and because we weren't close to any land mass, they…didn't think you'd survived…'

'And yet you continued to search for me? Even when everyone else thought I had perished? Why?' His piercing gaze drilled into her. As if seeking his own, deeper meaning for her actions. As if it *mattered* that she'd gone against everyone's belief that he'd perished.

Although she shrugged it was heavy with her own emotions. Yes, it would've been easier to accept that he was gone and got on with her life. But regardless of how they'd come together, she hadn't despised Zeph enough to readily accept that he'd died. And the searing abruptness of his disappearance had staggered her. Despite the video evidence, some immoveable stone of belief deep inside had rejected the idea that the formidable man whose name she reluctantly bore was gone.

'Your iron will terrifies most people. It just… didn't seem possible that you'd died just because you'd gone off the side of a boat. And if anyone could defy the impossible, it was you.' Because the statement sounded much too emotionally weighted, she hurried to add, 'Plus you were a very strong swimmer.' Watching him use the pool at their Athens apartment every morning had shown her that.

Imogen didn't realise she was wringing her hands until warm fingers crossed over hers. Startled she looked down.

'I didn't mean to distress you,' he rasped, then raised her hands to his lips. 'Your belief is why I'm here today, *glikia mou*. I will never forget that.'

She attempted an offhand shrug, which jerked a little, betraying her true, intensely ruffled feelings. 'It wasn't an easy situation. I can tell you that. Especially when unsavoury rumours started.' Her small attempt at humour came away a little starched, filled with tension.

His eyes narrowed. 'You were blamed for it?'

'The circumstances of our marriage lent themselves to the perfect tale of a gold-digger doing away with her husband so she could inherit his billions. Nobody knew who I was before you sent out a press release about our marriage. I was the daughter of a man you had some dealings with that nobody in Greece had even heard of. The media had a field day. Without the security footage, I would've probably been in serious trouble.'

Displeasure flashed over his face, and Imogen felt something kick inside her at the thought that he didn't immediately concur with what the authorities had heavily hinted at. That she was responsible for her husband's disappearance.

'Anyway, we searched for you for weeks. I hired a security firm that specialised in such matters three months later when it seemed the police were not getting anywhere. We've been scouring the globe for you ever since.'

Another smile ghosted over his lips, but it was the thumb trailing back and forth over her knuckles that made her emotions skitter all over the place. That made her own fingers itch to curl around his, draw his warmth into her. Because in that moment it struck Imogen that she didn't remember the last time anyone had touched her like this in a simple gesture of human warmth.

She barely remembered the mother who'd passed away when she was still a toddler, and the parade of nannies her father had employed hadn't felt inclined to coddle the child whose father had stated loudly that he wished her to be something she wasn't.

'Your tenacity paid off in the end. You have my thanks again.'

She breathed through the bite of guilt that scythed through the warmth.

As for the foreboding that tingled over her nape a second later, she had no remedy for it. But she would do what she had done since she was a child. She would battle whatever came and she would overcome it.

The sound of an approaching boat put paid to the difficult conversation and the unsettling sensations.

Imogen breathed a sigh of relief, then lost all her cool again when Zeph's touch lingered for several long seconds before transferring to the small of her back to guide her towards their approaching guest.

It was mildly amusing to see the small, rotund jeweller do a double take when he spotted Zeph.

'Mr Diamandis,' he exclaimed. 'I had no idea! No idea at all. Well, this is wonderful indeed,' he added, his gaze swinging wildly between Imogen and Zeph.

'Thank you, but I trust you will keep this news to yourself?' Zeph insisted.

The man's head bobbed several times. 'Of course, of course!'

His gaze swung between them for another few seconds before, reminded of the purpose of his visit, he extended the large briefcase handcuffed to his wrist. 'Is this a special occasion…? What am I saying? Of course it is! Would madam like to take a look at the selection?'

Zeph nudged Imogen towards the table where the jeweller had started to set out his collection but he answered, 'This is for me. I require a wedding ring.'

The shorter man's eyes widened, then a touch of regret darted over his face as he glanced up. 'Had I known you were…' He shook his head and cleared his throat. 'I've brought a selection but I can make sure you see the fuller collection. Maybe I can arrange for that to be brought to you tomorrow?'

Zeph shook his head. 'Show me what you have.'

The jeweller nodded enthusiastically and pulled out a black velvet tray studded with dozens of wedding rings. Zeph studied the array for a minute before midnight-blue eyes shifted to her. 'Imogen? Which do you prefer?'

Her startled eyes flew to his. 'Me? You want me to choose?'

His gaze dropped to her left hand. 'Did I choose yours?'

'Um…yes.'

'Then you will choose mine,' he said simply.

She wasn't going to tell him that part of the decision for the stunning ring set that adorned her finger was simply statement-making. The other part had been expediency. The jeweller, who had been there for her selection the day before they married, smiled in a way that made her think that he was reading a far too romantic connotation behind Zeph's request.

As to what her husband was thinking, she chose not to probe too deeply.

Staring down at the display, she dismissed the heavy gold bands and the super-thin titanium ones that were all the rage. She cast a discreet glance at Zeph's hands, the long, slightly callused capable fingers with a thick broad palm.

Her gaze zeroed in on a brushed platinum band with a row of tiny black diamonds dissecting the middle and her heart skipped a beat. Even before she reached for it, Imogen knew that it was the one. Hoping he wouldn't see the slight tremble in her hand as she reached for it, she drew it from its slot and held it out to him.

Zeph shook his head. Then slowly he extended his left hand to her, fingers outstretched. 'You do it,' he instructed thickly.

It was all so surreal.

As if she were caught up in a secret fantasy she couldn't extricate herself from even while her rational mind knew that it was a scene that would never come true.

But once again she was faced with a situation she couldn't refuse. So, sliding her fingers beneath his, Imogen slid the wedding ring onto her husband's finger. It settled easily and snugly, as if it was meant to be, and her breath caught over again as she saw it there, resting against his tanned skin.

With a compulsion she couldn't deny, she glanced up at him to find burnished flame heating his midnight-blue eyes. Eyes that seared hers for several moments, then dropped hungrily to her lips. And stayed.

The heavy sigh from the romantic jeweller was an effective sound that shattered the far too charged atmosphere. Dropping her hands, she aimed a smile at the short man. 'Thank you so much for coming on such short notice.'

He shook his head and waved her away. 'Anything for you, Mr and Mrs Diamandis. I'm only glad I was able to be of service.'

His hand dropping to his side, Zeph nodded at the hovering crew member. 'Goodnight. You will be seen out.'

As the man was escorted off the deck, she turned to find Zeph examining the ring on his finger. Moments later he looked up at her, and pinned her with his gaze.

'Now you have a means to find me should I ever stray from your side.'

They were matter-of-fact words, a practical solution to something that would probably never happen again. And yet her foolish heart leapt again. Unnerving her with the notion that a change was happening she *shouldn't* want and yet couldn't seem to stop herself from responding to.

She was still grappling with that growing problem when he placed his hand on the small of her back again and led her off the deck.

Realising that they were heading downstairs to the staterooms, Imogen scrambled to gird her loins for what was coming next.

Another debate about the sleeping arrangements? Or an interrogation about why they were sleeping apart in the first place.

But once again, he took the wind out of her sails by pausing in the hallway. 'Which one is yours?' he asked, indicating the stateroom doors.

She looked up, surprised, and he smiled. 'I'm not going to push myself on you or assert my marital rights, if that is what you're expecting.'

Because he had a headache or his instincts were reminding him that there had been no attraction between them before?

When one hand rose to clutch the back of his neck, Imogen abandoned trying to work it out. 'Two doors down,' she murmured.

With a curt nod, he led her to her door and turned the handle. After several seconds spent tracking every inch of her space, he turned to her.

'*Kalinychta, matia mou.* Sleep well. Tomorrow is another day.'

She watched him walk away, the dull thudding of her heart taunting her with the notion that she had expected a different outcome. Shaking her head, she shut the door and slowly walked across the carpet to her dressing room.

Her senses were still darting all over the place as she disrobed and slipped on her silk dressing down. Eyeing her bed, she knew sleep would be out of reach, at least for the moment, so she turned on her laptop and tackled the many items on her perpetually full to-do list.

An hour later she stood and stretched her back, a little irritated with herself when she noted that sleep was still out of reach. Going to bed would only result in tossing and turning and getting more annoyed.

She toyed with calling for a cup of chamomile tea and discarded the idea, settling instead for a glass of cold water from the chilled cabinet that contained an assortment of drinks in her room.

The small private balcony attached to her stateroom beckoned with the promise of fresh air. Opening the door, she stepped out, sighing at the cool marble floor beneath her feet and the light breeze that soothed her heated skin.

It wasn't so much a noise as it was a keen awareness that made her glance to the side. All notions of relaxation or quieting her thoughts enough to sleep evaporated when she spotted Zeph.

He was bent over at the waist, wearing nothing but dark silk pyjama bottoms, elbows on the railing while his thumbs dug into his temples. He hadn't seen her yet, probably because long strands of his hair obstructed his view. Calling herself shameless and a few other derogatory names didn't stop her from ogling his beautifully muscled torso. His trim waist. The perfect symmetry from head to toe.

Then worrying about his obvious distress.

Turn away. Go back to bed.

Resignedly, she wasn't alarmed when her feet wouldn't move. Nor was she surprised when his head swung towards her a second later, his hands falling away from his head when he saw her.

For several seconds, they stared at one another across the small expanse of dark, swirling water that separated their balconies.

'You're having trouble sleeping too.' It wasn't a question but an even observation.

She dragged her gaze from the wisps of silky hair that trailed down his chest and disappeared into his pyjama bottoms. Myriad excuses rose to her lips, but in the end she just shrugged. 'Like you said, a lot has happened today. It's a lot to process.'

He gave a solemn nod, his gaze taking her in

from head to toe before reconnecting with her eyes again. The atmosphere thickened between them until her heartbeat thudded in her ears.

'Is your headache still bothering you?' she asked before she could bite her tongue.

The corner of his mouth crooked. 'I don't think it's going anywhere any time soon.'

She didn't realise her feet were moving until she was at the far end of her railing closest to his. He too had wandered close as he spoke. She only needed to stretch out her hand to touch him.

Not that she wanted to, she assured herself.

Her fingers tightened around her glass as she watched him massage his temples again.

Don't do it. Don't!

But her heart rate was rising and that soft part of her heart was loosening even further.

'Let me help,' she offered before she could change her mind. 'My grandfather suffered from headaches. They were mostly migraines but if what you're feeling is even close...' Her voice trailed away as his eyes zeroed in on her in that ferociously specific way again. That way that alarmed her into believing he could read her every thought, decipher her every emotion.

Breath held, Imogen stood there suspended in strange expectation.

After an age, he nodded. Then he did something completely unexpected.

Reaching out, he touched a switch on the wall next to him. She gasped as the balcony slid smoothly sideways, a part of it seamlessly unfolding to latch on to and meld with his.

Zeph looked as surprised as she did.

'Did you know that was there?' she asked.

He shook his head, a little bemused. 'Not consciously. I guess muscle memory just kicked in.'

Her heart stuttered. 'That's good, I guess?' Her voice wobbled because in that moment she knew this might be the way his memories returned. Between one thought and the next. One unconscious gesture and another.

Staring thoughtfully at the button, he nodded, oblivious to her suddenly rioting emotions. 'It can't hurt.'

And then his gaze was returning to her, his left hand extending to help her across the short distance. Their gazes fell on his new ring at the same time and that peculiar sensation kicked hard inside her again.

The fantasy whipped up, teasing her with possibilities she had never let herself entertain in the almost two years she'd been Mrs Diamandis. Because it'd been useless.

They were enemies.

Her family had ruined his a long time ago and,

to this day, Zeph suffered nightmares about it. Nightmares he had no clue how to decipher.

Pushing the guilty morsel of thought away, she followed him into his room.

Avoiding looking at his rumpled bed was impossible. Which triggered images of him lying between the sheets, his sleek limbs sprawled out in masculine splendour.

No, she wasn't going to think that way. The day had been fraught with pitfalls already. She wasn't going to invite more.

Then why are you here, offering assistance, when you could be in the safety of your room?

She told herself it was a good thing that she hadn't lost her humanity. But the voice continued to tease her as she walked across the opulent space to the sprawling sofa sets on one side of his stateroom.

'How do you want me?' he drawled.

Every awakened cell in her body jumped. 'Um…what?'

His lips quirked. 'Where is this going to happen, Imogen?' he amended, amusement trailing through his discomfort.

'Oh. Um…' She ignored the heat devouring her face and pointed to the largest sofa. 'If you stretch out on there I can work on your neck.'

He nodded and immediately strode across the room to the seat.

Watching him lie face down, his torso bronzed and stretched in confident abandon, made her tongue swell in her mouth. Hunger like she'd never known before rippled through her belly, making her breath pant lightly.

Good God, what was wrong with her?

Shaking her head and feverishly praying the sensation would disappear, she set her glass down and approached him.

The sofa was large enough to accommodate a six-foot-three man and to allow her to perch alongside him without discomfort. Unfortunately, it didn't allow too much of a separation between them and Imogen discovered the precarious position she had put herself in when her hip nudged his the moment she sat down.

She swallowed, determined not to be bothered by the heated proximity. She was here to ease his suffering, not indulge in the torrid images flashing across her brain.

Get yourself together, she berated herself.

Breathing out, she swept his long hair out of the way and planted her fingers at the base of his neck. Heat from his skin flowed into hers and, for the wildest moments, every thought in her head evaporated, save for the sensation she wanted to indulge in.

No.

She kneaded his flesh, studiously recalling

how she had treated her grandfather when he'd suffered. The side of Zeph's neck was knotted in tense muscles. She concentrated her efforts there, using firm circular motions that drew a muted grunt from him. Absurdly pleased with that sound, she worked harder, leaning in when he didn't reject her firmer efforts. He groaned when she reached his hairline and Imogen hid a smile. Working from one side to the other and then concentrating on both sides in concert, she worked his muscles loose, then returned to his shoulders.

'I was wrong,' his voice rambled, his speech slightly slurred as he leaned into her touch. 'I don't believe in the occult, but I suspect yours are magical hands.'

This time she couldn't suppress the wide smile that broke out. 'I like winning. I especially relish proving you wrong.'

A sound rumbled out of him, a cross between a groan and laughter.

'Well, I will admit all the wrongs in the world if you keep going,' he promised.

Companionable silence filled the room as she concentrated on her efforts and was rewarded with several more sounds of appreciation. After half an hour, she sat back and rested her hands in her lap.

'Now for the temples.'

He raised his head and looked at her over his shoulder. One eyebrow quirked, an expression that could've been interpreted as surprise pleasure on his face. 'There's more?'

Imogen ignored the leaping of her heart and the tightening in her pelvis and nodded. 'It worked for Grandpa,' she threw in, just to dilute what was happening to her.

Zeph shrugged. 'If it was good enough for your grandfather...'

He turned over with lithe animal grace, and then simply watched her, waiting for instruction.

She gestured with her hand. 'I need to be behind you.'

He nodded and rose to sit upright. This close, his scent was unavoidable. Sandalwood and warm, vibrant skin, it invited her to breathe him in long and deep. And because her senses were totally overwhelmed by a full day she still hadn't fully taken in, Imogen gave up fighting it.

Positioning herself behind him, she waited until he leaned back, half on the seat and half against her. Charges shot up and down her body as his naked torso rested against her chest.

She had gone past the point of worrying whether this was a good idea or not. Right now, the only thing she needed to do was to help him, and then return to her room. As soon as possible.

But touching his shoulder when he was facing

away from her was one thing. With their faces almost aligned, it was impossible to work on him without taking in the sheer perfection of Zeph's features.

And when at her first touch, his eyes drifted shut, she did just that.

As he had done to her for every single moment today, she watched him with unashamed avidness as she drew circular motions on his temple and down to his jaw. In incremental degrees, the tightness in his face dissolved, his tension ebbing away and his breathing evening out.

When he muttered something under his breath in Greek, Imogen smiled.

'I don't know whether you've worked it out yet but I don't speak Greek.'

A ghost of a smile whispered over his lips but his eyes remained shut. 'Hmm, then I'll have to teach you.'

After several moments ticked by, she opened her mouth to prompt him to translate what he had said before but then she saw that he'd fallen asleep.

Since his weight wasn't fully on her, she wasn't crushed. On the contrary, it felt…pleasant. Intimate. Despite it being only physical, it was a connection she hadn't experienced…ever.

Her heart lurched with the craving that arose from that knowledge, the need to extend it, if

only for a little while. Her hands continued to
rub against his temples, soothing him even in
sleep. And then she moved her fingers into his
hair, pushing firmly against his scalp.

He groaned in his sleep, leaning harder into
her touch.

Her heart lurched, emotion she couldn't explain
rising into her throat. Was she really doing this?
Falling under whatever spell this was?

He was asleep now. She had done what she
came to do. She should leave.

And yet she stayed, her fingers working away
for long minutes, occasionally gliding through
his silky hair.

When they began to cramp, she moved them
to rest on his shoulders.

For another handful of minutes she contem-
plated how to extricate herself from him without waking him. His head was wedged firmly
between her breasts and one arm thrown over
her thighs.

Taking a breath, she slid a few inches. Then
another few.

Then gave a short gasp as Zeph adjusted,
turned sideways and threw both arms around her.

For several seconds Imogen stopped breathing. She glanced desperately at the door leading
to the balcony. And then down at the man trap-
ping her against him.

She was wide awake and she doubted sleep would come any time soon. So where was the harm in staying and letting him achieve a little bit of peace before moving?

Several warnings, mostly of the foolishness of her thought pattern, rushed into her brain. One by one she discarded them, her heart thumping wildly as she gave in and settled back against the sofa.

One hour, she promised herself. Another hour for the man she had relentlessly searched for for endless months. He deserved a good night's sleep. Besides, if it helped him regain his memory that much quicker, wasn't that a good thing?

Nodding solemnly to herself, she drew her fingers through his hair one last time and then dropped her own head against the fat cushions.

One hour.

Except when she opened her eyes, she was no longer on the sofa, and it wasn't night-time any longer.

The sun was blazing past the half-opened shades in the room.

And she was in bed with her husband.

And not just in bed. She was wrapped tight in his arms, her face tucked into a warm, naked shoulder and one arm thrown over his waist.

Her lungs emptied, her whole body stiffening as she looked up. And up.

Into the face of a wide-awake Zeph, who was staring at her with unabashed interest.

CHAPTER SIX

THE EVER-PRESENT FRICTION that relentlessly marked their interactions shot up by a thousand degrees the moment their eyes met. Like a flame tossed onto gasoline, Imogen felt it light a path down their connected bodies, extinguishing what little brain power and oxygen there was left in the room.

'*Kalismera*, Imogen,' Zeph rasped.

A shudder as every cell sizzled at his deep, languid voice.

Move. Speak. Do something.

Anticipating her body's reluctance to obey, she forcibly disentangled herself and pushed at his shoulders. He resisted for a nanosecond before his arms loosened.

Rolling away from him, she dragged her gaze from his naked, *delicious* torso, a jagged kind of relief slithering through her when she saw she was still in her bathrobe, although the belt had come seriously loose.

'Wh-what am I doing here?' she asked, cringing at the breathless quality of her voice as she tightened the belt.

Zeph's shoulder hitched in a languid shrug. 'The sofa is comfortable only for so long. I didn't want you to wake up with a sore neck, so I moved you.'

'But you could've woken me up.'

'Why? You were struggling to sleep as much as I was. It was clear you needed it. No harm no foul.' A moment ticked by. Then two. His jaw tightened. 'Or do you think there was foul, *glikia mou*?' he enquired silkily, in that way that sent different kinds of shivers down her spine.

She raised a hand to drag back her dishevelled hair, then bit back a moan when the act reminded her how very little she was wearing beneath the robe. Reminded how that very thin scrap of fabric had been the only thing between their bodies.

How that sparked new, eager flames in her.

She was scrambling to place more distance between herself and that thought when he jack-knifed upright.

'A lesser man would develop a complex from your reactions. Which is puzzling because you're attracted to me.' When she opened her mouth to issue a hot denial, he batted it away. 'Your body gives you away, Imogen.'

She didn't need to glance down to confirm his statement. The tips of her breasts were hard and aching, screaming and displaying their need to him.

'Which makes me think the reluctance is…' His jaw clenched tight for a moment before he shook his head. Narrow-eyed, his expression changed from lazy cynicism to fierce intent. 'Was I cruel to you?' The words were bitten out, as if he didn't want to say them, but needed to know.

Her heart lurched, both at the fire in his eyes and the sensation of shifting sands beneath her feet. 'You weren't abusive, if that's what you're asking.'

His nostrils flared and he dragged a hand through his own hair. 'You know what I'm asking, Imogen.'

She sucked in a breath. Then shook her head. 'You weren't cruel in the true sense of the word. But you were…indifferent. I was a means to an end for you.'

He stiffened. 'Why? And why you?'

Please don't make me answer that.

She breathed a short-lived sigh of relief when the plea didn't tumble out. But she still needed to answer. 'I asked you the same thing when you… when my father told me about the deal he was making with you.'

His gaze probed deeper. 'Your father? He was involved in arranging our union somehow?'

She wanted to laugh. Both at the understatement and at the way Zeph oh-so-accurately referred to their marriage as a negotiation even though he had no memory of it. 'Yes. From start to finish.'

'And?'

'And…you said you preferred to enter an agreement with a clear understanding that there would be zero emotional involvement between us.'

'Why?' he breathed.

'I don't know.'

'You're an intelligent woman, Imogen. You had an idea. Give me your best guess.'

Dear God, this was not the conversation she'd expected to have with Zeph first thing in the morning. But then, hadn't the last twenty-four hours been the most intensely peculiar of her life?

'From what the media speculated on from your private life before we married, you didn't date the same woman for more than a few months. And more than one of those women gossiped that while you were…' she paused, licked dry lips '…generous with your time and attention up to a point, you weren't the romantic type. And in an interview when you were younger you stated that you would win a bet against anyone who claimed that any woman who dated a wealthy man didn't have an ulterior, long-term motive.'

His expression didn't change but she sensed a shift in the air, perhaps even a whisper of bewilderment. Or was she fooling herself? His hardening face moments later said perhaps she was.

'I sense it's the sort of conclusion someone with first-hand experience reaches,' he drawled.

Stung by the biting admission, she shrugged. 'I wouldn't know.'

Dark blue eyes pinned her in place. 'Had we met before this…agreement between us was struck?'

She shook her head, her breath frozen in her lungs. 'No. But you were acquainted with my father. And if you're wondering so, no, I wasn't your type.'

He rolled onto his knees with the agility and grace of a panther, the motion rendering her immobile as he reached out and wrapped his large hand around her jaw and nape.

'And exactly what do you think is my type?' he enquired in a low, deep bedroom voice that steeped the charged atmosphere.

'Heiresses. Supermodels. Daughters of presidents. Some of the most beautiful women in the world have called themselves your lovers.'

His eyes narrowed a fraction. 'You alluded to that yesterday. And I recall responding that this past you seem intrigued with didn't stop me from putting a ring on your finger. From giving you my name.'

'No…you…'

His grip tightened a fraction as if imprinting his words into her skin. 'I am a powerful man. And I am not unintelligent. I believe I have several recourses to any situation I face. Think about that when you wonder why I chose you.'

No. The protest shrieked louder inside her. Because to take him at his word meant…

'Why do you want this? Why do you want me?' The words ripped from somewhere deep inside her, a peculiar, secret yearning rearing its head that wouldn't be silenced.

The question seemed to momentarily startle him as much as it startled her. Then that formidable self-assuredness reasserted itself. 'Because you're the first woman to evoke such an…interesting reaction in me since I woke up in Efemia,' he drawled.

'And that's it? I *interest* you? What's to say you won't find the next woman who walks onto this deck equally interesting?'

His eyes narrowed. 'I did *not* cheat on you.'

The certainty with which he stated that dropped like an anvil on them both. 'No.'

'Then do not insult me by suggesting that I would be so fickle.'

She cursed the flush that damned her in that moment. 'You were about to marry another woman when I found you.'

It spoke volumes to the imperious nature of her husband that he accepted that tossed-out argument with a mere inclination of his head. 'True. But if it reassures you she didn't interest me as much as you do, and I'm confident she was only marrying me for her own motives.'

'Did you…propose to her?' Why was that so important to her? Why did it make her heart stutter to even think of Zeph going down on one knee to another?

'Not in traditional terms. There was a general, informal discussion, which then seemed to take on a life of its own.'

'What does that mean?'

'It means out of the three people involved, Petros was the most keen on the marriage happening.'

As she recalled the older man's hostility when she'd interrupted his daughter's wedding, Imogen's fists bunched on her thighs.

Zeph's gaze dropped to them before rising. 'Why, my dear, you look positively livid,' he said with a musing smile.

She breathed out slowly, willed the discordant thoughts into composure. 'I'm not…it's just…'

In the last five minutes, he'd made statements on which he didn't have sufficient information to make. And yet each time, her soul had leapt. The insane cravings in her heart had lapped them up like starved soil receiving rain.

And within those cravings, Imogen recognised her old self, the child who'd desperately wanted that lavish, healing rain. Wanted so much for her father to *see* her, acknowledge her. *Love* her. The same way this new, oblivious Zeph seemed intent on convincing her she could have the impossible.

Yes, he'd been thrust into an old world he didn't remember, but not once had he struck her as helpless. And yet...last night he'd *needed* her. He'd listened to her. Was perhaps even reluctant to let her out of his sight. As much as she wanted to cite feminism and independence, she'd never felt anything like this before. Never craved this feeling with this much desperation. So, while terrifying, was it wrong to bask in it for just a little...?

Yes.

She accepted the shrieked internal warning and forced a laugh, a desperate attempt to lighten the mood thickening around them, threatening tsunami-sized waves of sensation she wasn't sure she was ready for. 'Put yourself in my shoes. Tell me how you would've reacted to that.'

'If it makes you feel better, I would've been positively incandescent. I would've thrown you over my shoulder and carried you away like a caveman. Then I would've spent the next month locked in this bedroom with you beneath me, reminding you who you belonged to,' he stated with a voice coated in pure, unadulterated erotic promise.

Her jaw sagged. Her pulse leaped. Her breath shortened.

He laughed, a rich, decadent sound that tunnelled deep, heating her core, dragging even more sensation to the surface until she feared she would drown in it.

'But since the shoe is on the other foot and my wife seems to be skittish about our reacquaintance, I'll endeavour to take it slow.'

She moved a little too late, her limbs rebelling against denying her body what it craved. She'd only made it to the end of the bed when he huffed out a breath.

'There you go, running away again.' The words were tinged with frustration.

Imogen stilled, knowing she should absolutely *not* rise to the bait. And yet, God, he drove her beyond rational thought.

She crawled back onto the bed and glared him down. 'Fine. Here I am, staying right here. Do your worst.'

The moment the impetuous words were out of her mouth, she wanted to snatch them back. Because they were as blatant as dangling a juicy chunk of meat under a lion's nose and expecting him not to bite her hand off with it.

And when that infernal, wickedly devastating smile started to unravel over his sinful face, she knew she was well and truly trapped. 'My worst? No, *glikia mou*. What you'll be receiving from me won't be my worst but my very best.'

Before she could stop shivering long enough to ask what he meant, he was curling a firm arm around her waist, drawing her close until their bodies were plastered together.

He didn't immediately dive in for the kiss she realised every cell in her body was anticipating. His gaze raked her face, the pulse leaping at her throat, the frantic rise and fall of her chest. Savouring the reaction he drew so effortlessly from her.

That was all the warning she received before he drew her even closer, and sealed his lips over hers.

It started off as a replay of that fizzle of electricity she'd felt when they'd kissed back in the apartment in Athens. Then almost immediately it escalated in sensation, growing wild and untamed when his tongue breached the seams of lips she'd parted willingly, her resistance crumbling almost as soon as she felt that erotic probe.

And… God…it was sublime.

A moan slipped free before she could stop it, her hands rising to trail up his bare, thick, hot arms to rest at his nape, a willing companion on this insane ride that had her straining onto her tiptoes, eager for more even before she'd taken her first, desperate breath.

He kissed like a man forged for lovemaking. And yes, her own experiences weren't nearly adequate enough to know a good kisser from a mediocre one. All she knew was that Zeph, her *husband*, kissed like a maestro. And she was a willing, eager pupil.

That tongue swept in deeper and shamelessly caressed hers. A cracked moan ended in a whimper and when he tightened his hold, she trembled at the overwhelming pleasure that swept through her.

If it makes you feel better, I would've been positively incandescent.

Absurdly, it did make her feel better, which probably also made her a cavewoman. But she chose to keep that to herself. Choosing instead to glide her hands up and over his shoulders, caressing the skin and muscle she'd touched in a different capacity last night, scouring lightly with her nails and revelling in the shudder that went through him.

'*Ne*, just like that.'

His throaty encouragement spurred her on to greater madness. She nipped at his bottom lip, revelling in the hiss that broke free before he grunted in approval and returned the favour in erotic bites that had her knees sagging as pleasure weakened her limbs.

In the next moment, he was turning her, urging her backwards. When the pillows met her back, she welcomed it, her thighs parting eagerly to accommodate the man who stared down at her with ferocious hunger and single-minded intent before bearing down on her, accepting the space she made for him.

The kiss that followed was even more decadent, wetter, hungrier, their tongues duelling for supremacy in pleasure granting and receiving.

'*Theós*, you taste sublime,' he muttered hoarsely, his lips freeing hers to explore her jaw and neck, inhaling deeply before catching one earlobe between his teeth. 'I'm barely holding myself back from devouring you.'

Another helpless moan tore free, the sound triggering even more desperation in the need clamouring through her. She spiked her fingers in his hair and dragged his mouth back to hers, eager to experience more of the sensational magic they created together.

He acceded to her wish, after another rumble of male laughter that said he was pleased with her febrile reaction.

The first inkling she had that her robe was once again loose was when his hot lips trailed over one upper slope of her breast, flicked with teasing strokes over the tight nub before latching to suck her flesh into his mouth.

Her back bowed, pleasure searing her from head to toe before concentrating with sharp saturation between her thighs. 'Oh, God!'

She clenched her fists in his hair, unable to decide whether she craved more or needed relief. Zeph was intent on more, of course, his fingers tormenting the other peak until only incoherent sounds spilled from her lips.

Her eyes rolled shut when he continued the tormenting journey down her belly to the edge of the tiny thong she wore.

When his fingers snagged in the fabric and dragged it down her legs, Imogen suspected what was coming. Mild dismay dulled the edges of her pleasure. She'd only experienced oral sex once, with disastrous results she never wanted to repeat. So when Zeph gripped her thighs and tried to nudge them apart, she resisted.

'I don't… I'm not…are you sure you want to do this?'

His gaze pinned hers. 'You don't want it?'

An anticipatory shudder wove through her even as misgivings lingered. 'I do, but…'

'You don't believe I'll make it good for you?' The question was heavy with so much arrogance, she wondered why he was bothering to enquire. And since she couldn't seem to adequately string words together, he conceitedly continued, 'Be assured, wife. I will drive you out of your mind.'

With that, he pried her legs apart, dropped that sublime body low, and swept his tongue in one bold stroke over her femininity that had her biting her fist and moaning in delirium. Shamelessly, Zeph parted her thighs wider.

And feasted.

Thoroughly. Relentlessly. Ravenously.

Until her moans were one long fevered song, a melody in praise of his mastery he punctuated with thick Greek words as he drove her to the peak of desire. And when they grew sharp and desperate, he brought his fingers into play, stroking them deep into her heated channel as he doubled his efforts on the bundle of nerves crowning her core.

Imogen lost all sense of time and space as bliss enslaved her, held her tight in rhapsody before tossing her over the peak.

She tumbled with a piercing scream, her fingers scrambling for purchase in the long and mindless descent. From a fragment of awareness, she realised the thing she clung to was Zeph. His hands, then his shoulders as he kissed his way back up her body. As he sealed her lips with a kiss that was decadent, wicked and unabashed in its hunger.

And when she blinked her eyes open several minutes later and realised they'd, either mystically or by coincidence, returned to the clasp they'd been in when she'd woken, Imogen tried not to panic. Not to be overwhelmed by the ever-thickening layers of sensations and emotions buffeting her.

He kissed with ever-growing hunger, and, desperate not to be sucked under again, Imogen returned the caress for a minute, then firmly took charge, striking out on her own journey. She ignored his grunt of disapproval when she ended the kiss, then hid a smile when she nipped his jaw and dropped kisses on his strong throat.

Did she have any firm idea what she was doing? Maybe not. Her handful of sexual encounters had been little more than furtive fumbles in the dark, over too quickly for her to catalogue what true pleasure entailed.

But Zeph wasn't displeased, so, heart in her throat, she licked her way down his chest and grazed her teeth over flat male nipples that had a full body shudder rippling through him. A quick glance up showed his hands gripping the pillow and his eyes rabidly fixed on her.

'*Ne,*' he breathed. 'More.'

The hoarse encouragement empowered her, loosening her inhibitions as she explored his six-pack with her hands and mouth, then journeyed the short distance south to the waistband of his pyjama bottoms.

Seeing her hesitation, Zeph reared up and drew the garment down and off, tossing it away without taking his eyes off her, then lying back down.

Imogen felt a little faint at the first sight of his manhood. Dear God, no wonder he exuded such arrogance! No wonder he believed he was the king of the world.

'Cease the torture, *yineka mou*,' he implored.

She licked her lips, and closed her mouth over him, glorying in the shout that ripped from his lips. A moment later, the hands grasping the pillows knotted in her hair, directing her as she lavished attention on his hot, thick manhood.

Decadent sounds filled the room, awakening her own arousal. At her moan, Zeph cursed, his eyes mere slits of blazing arousal as he watched her ministrations.

'I should marry you again,' he mused thickly, his fingers knotting tighter in her hair, then groaning as her tongue lapped his rigid length. 'Reinforce my claim on you so no other man has any ideas of taking what's mine.'

A drop of ice slithered down her spine, followed immediately by a few more. Still she kept her grip on him, the craving churning inside fighting the thunderbolt he'd casually dropped at her feet.

'Wh-what?' she stammered.

The small puff of air produced by her demand washed over his member, making him groan again. 'You heard me. And don't stop,' he growled.

Even as her brain grappled between elation at what he'd said and the reality that it could never happen, she was tempted to keep on caressing him.

But loosening the hold on her emotions was what had led to this in the first place. And every moment she spent in this false nirvana was another moment she'd have to account for later.

Imogen told herself she was glad common sense won out. That things had gone too far too quickly. 'No.'

The air stilled around them. Neither of them breathed after that firm rejection.

His fingers disentangled from her hair. She realised she was still gripping him when he took hold of her wrist and decisively pushed her away.

And it shamed her that she mourned the loss of him as he withdrew from her, his face hardening as he stood and tugged his bottoms back on.

He took a single step from her and Imogen barely stopped herself from swaying towards him, a pliant flower straining towards the sun's warmth.

'No?' The query was as icy and forbidding as his set jaw.

She swallowed, scrambled for some semblance of shattered control. 'No, that's not going to happen. You seem to think any objection I have is a challenge or an affront. Have you stopped to think I may not want the same thing as you?'

His mouth twitched with empty humour. 'Here's your chance, then. Tell me what's so objectionable about remarrying your husband.'

Snatching her robe off the bed, she fought her way into it, cinching the belt tight. 'Among other things? You've been back less than twenty-four hours!'

He jerked out a nod. 'Granted. If time is what you need we can discuss it. What are the other objections?'

'Are you serious? We shouldn't even have done…what we just did,' she said, waving a frantic hand at the rumpled bed.

'For a woman with a healthy appetite such as yours, you seem hell-bent on self-flagellation at the earliest sign of displaying desire. Hide behind obstacles if you wish, but I still want an answer.'

Words crowded on her tongue. Words she couldn't speak without bringing down this precarious house of cards they'd built to maintain the status quo.

'I'm waiting, dear wife. Why did you bother to keep looking for me? From what I've seen since my return you were the only one actively doing so,' he stated bitterly. 'While you've given me glimpses of what this marriage of ours entailed, your attitude goes against everything rational. You could've left me to rot, forgotten on that sleepy island. Why didn't you?'

'Because I didn't want to wait seven years!'

He stilled at the words that ripped free without her permission, his whole body a frozen column of marble, like one of those celebrated Greek gods. Eyes like the ocean's depths pinned her where she knelt. 'Explain,' he demanded, his tone still gruff but cooling at a fast rate. 'Now.'

Mildly nauseous at what she'd let slip, Imogen sagged onto the bed. But reminded of just who she was dealing with, she immediately straightened her spine. She wasn't quite ready to look him in the eye though, so she focused her gaze on some middle point in the room. 'The general consensus from the lawyers was that if you weren't found I'd have to wait seven years to have you declared dead. I… I didn't want that hanging over my head.'

'Again. Why? You already have an exulted place on the board and my billions at your disposal—'

'It wasn't about money or my place on the board! It was about my life. My freedom.'

That marble effect encompassed his face. Abstractly, Imogen marvelled at how breathtaking he looked.

'Your *freedom*? From me?'

Numbly, she nodded.

He inhaled sharply. 'So let me see if I have this

right. Your plan was to find me, *and then divorce me*?' he breathed.

There was disbelief in the query. But also rumbling fury.

Which thankfully kicked up her own resistance.

She scrambled upright, ignoring the trembling in her body that was the residue of the lustful acts they'd committed on each other. Well, almost in his case. She grimaced inwardly and pulled in a long breath. But when she opened her mouth, she was reminded of the doctor's admonition and hesitated.

He saw it. His nostrils flared. And even before he opened his mouth, she knew what was coming. 'Do not even think about withholding from me. I won't hesitate to summon every single employee, board member and acquaintance to interrogate one by one until I get to the truth. A truth I'm suspecting we both agreed to keep under wraps for whatever reason?'

'Fine. You want to know why? Part of the agreement we made when we married was that either or both of us had the option to petition for divorce after three years.'

He looked momentarily poleaxed. Then he shook his head. 'Impossible.'

'Oh, no, it isn't. And you were the one who put

it in the agreement. In fact, the whole agreement was drawn up by your lawyers.'

'And you're in a hurry to reach that point of separation because...' He paused, his gaze snapping volcanic fire. 'Is there someone else?' he demanded icily, his chest rising and falling with mesmerising pace. 'Who is he? That Harvard puppy sniffing around you?'

'No! But...that's what we agreed.'

Her jaw dropped when he whirled around. She watched him stride to where he'd discarded his mobile phone in the living area.

'What are you doing?'

He returned to the bedroom and held it out to her. 'You say there's an agreement. I'm finding out everything there is to it. Call my lawyer.'

Imogen knew there was no point arguing.

She had no one but herself to blame. She'd dropped a disconcerting fact into his life when she should've kept her mouth shut. Refusing his request now would only further exacerbate the problem.

Taking the phone, she brought up the website of the firm Zeph used for his private matters. She gave her name and was immediately connected. She handed the phone to Zeph and a second later he was delivering a torrent of Greek into the receiver. The conversation lasted less than three minutes before he hung up.

Without looking her way, he marched out of the room, then returned scant minutes later holding a sleek laptop.

'Sit down, Imogen.'

Dear God, what had she done?

She sat. Waited while he pulled up the document she was certain his lawyers had sent to him in record time. Narrow-eyed, he read through the agreement then slammed the machine shut. 'I have good news and bad news for you, my sweet,' he declared, that voice still wrapped in ice. 'From first glance at this agreement, I already see a few loopholes I can explore. If nothing else, it'll keep you busy...*and married* for longer than three years.'

Her heart jumped before dropping to her toes. 'Zeph...'

One corner of his lips quirked. 'It's a little too late to attempt to wrap me around your finger with that sexy voice.'

She gasped. 'I wasn't doing anything of the sort!'

His mouth quirked higher. 'Which makes this all the more promising. It will be delightful to see how far you resist what you truly want.'

'Excuse me? What's that supposed to mean—?'

'It means I have a new proposal for you. You will give me six months I'll never forget and I'll consider letting you go, as per our original agreement,' he interjected with titanium finality.

'Six months you'll never forget?' she echoed with a dry mouth, absolutely refusing to entertain the possible fireworks wrapped in those words. 'What does that entail, exactly?' she forced herself to demand.

His casual shrug did nothing to ease her mind. Not when his eyes glinted with Machiavellian shrewdness that made her belly quake. 'I am your long-lost husband returned from the dead. Who has felt a distinct…lack in his wife's enthusiasm.'

She expelled a breath shrouded in mild panic and lots of irritation. 'I've told you why.'

'And I expect you to do better.'

'You can't be serious! And if I don't?'

'Then you might be left wishing you'd waited seven years and washed your hands of me once and for all. And I might just insist we wait out however long my memory returns to get the full picture of the state of affairs.'

He rose and stared down at her. 'I suggest you think it through and have an answer ready for me by dinner tonight.' He turned and started to walk away.

And since some part of her insisted on compounding an already precarious position, she opened her mouth and damned herself some more. 'Where are you going?'

'To take care of the blue balls you've cursed me with. I suggest you not be here when I come out.'

Her face was flaming red by the time he set the laptop down and stalked off in the direction of the bathroom.

But that embarrassment was nothing compared to the blaze alight in her brain for what she'd just unleashed.

Try as he might, it turned out his hand was no compensation for the thrill of Imogen's mouth. Satisfaction was hard to come by—pun intended—when his head was reeling with what Imogen had finally disclosed to him.

Imogen.

The wife who was counting the minutes until she would be free of him.

With a thick curse, Zeph wrenched the shower tap from warm to cold, giving up on achieving any release. The voice that mocked him that he should've left things alone rose, gloating louder.

Six months.

To the possible end of a marriage he didn't recall entering into.

To the prospect that if…when she walked away from him, he would be as alone as he had been the night he'd woken up in a strange house on a strange isle, surrounded by strangers.

Six months to get this insane chemical reaction he felt for his wife out of his system. Perhaps he was on his way to full recovery of his memories.

Because, if his wife was to be believed and his previous liaisons were short-lived, then the six months he'd stipulated would be more than adequate. And if they were contracted to part then anyway…

Was he really so alarmed at the prospect of being alone that he was pushing for an intimacy that wasn't there? *No.* It was there. He'd felt it last night. She'd cared for him of her own free will. And he'd…enjoyed it. He was astute enough to know he had the power to dismantle, if not all, then *some* of her resistance. What was wrong with letting time and proximity work on the rest?

He had six months. Enough time to will his memories to return. Hell, that incident on the balcony had proved that it was only a matter of time. He'd bought himself time. Maybe even to seduce this reticent wife who believed she could resist the blinding chemistry between them. Either way, he would make progress while taking firmer control of his life.

Taking firmer control of his marriage.

And if he failed?

He gritted his teeth at the disagreeing churning in his gut and pushed the question away.

Turning off the tap, he stepped out of the shower, his mood nowhere near improved.

Rubbing the towel over his wet hair, he lowered his resistance against the probing argument that demanded attention. He might not know how he'd dealt with problems in his pre-amnesia life, but he'd discovered that allowing a problem to saturate his mind until he could dwell on very little else usually tossed up an answer. Like a full tide that had had no other option but to recede to sea once the moon called.

So…was something else at play here?

Was he using sex and forced companionship, this…attachment to cling to something that wasn't there? The events of the past day should've brought a measure of satisfaction. Instead, he felt just as unmoored as he had when he'd opened his eyes in that stranger's bed in Efemia ten months ago. Hell, in some ways he felt worse.

He'd returned home only to feel homeless.

He'd reunited with his wife only to feel more disconnected and alone than ever.

A billionaire stricken with a peculiar destitution he would've feared was soul-deep if he believed in spirituality.

And more than once yesterday, he'd experienced the sinking feeling that, even were his memories to return, he wouldn't shed these unwanted sensations that easily. That beyond the impressive successes attached to his name, Zephyr Diamandis the man was far from…content.

Of course, he wouldn't admit that to anyone.

He didn't need further pointers to know the

entirety of his achievements had come from being single-mindedly focused. Perhaps ruthless, too. And one didn't hang onto such laudable feats by admitting ephemeral nonsense and weaknesses. No.

One did something about it.

And the most obvious place to start was with Imogen.

With gritty determination, he went into his dressing room.

Perhaps he was being presumptuous. But since he didn't plan on losing...

He would take every second of that six months he'd bargained for himself. And, memory or no memory, perhaps it would be a good opportunity to get to the bottom of who he truly was.

He dressed, for the first time eschewing the shorts and T-shirts he'd grown fond of for a pair of white linen trousers and matching shirt. His bare feet he left alone. He liked feeling the movement of the sea beneath his soles. Liked the connection with his immediate past. Why change that if he didn't need to?

He ignored the dart of disappointment to see that Imogen had heeded his words and made herself scarce. Because he would've liked another tussle with her?

Deciding there was nothing wrong with that way of thinking, he left the stateroom. A crew member waiting in the hallway immediately stepped forward.

'Good morning, Mr Diamandis. Would you like some breakfast?'

'Yes.'

'Any preference as to where you want to take it, sir?'

'Where does my wife take hers?'

'The smaller dining room on Deck Four,' he replied.

'Then I'll dine there with her.'

'Very good, sir.'

When he continued to linger, Zeph exhaled. 'It's fine. You can go. I'll find my way there.'

The young lad sent him a small searching look before nodding, then hurried off.

Alone, Zeph lingered, closing his eyes and attempting to see if the muscle memory from last night would kick in again. After a full minute of nothing happening, he gritted his teeth and opened his eyes.

But as he climbed the stairs to the deck, something rushed to the forefront of his mind, something that had struck him when he'd risen this morning and then been buried under the sensual deluge of tangling with his wife.

For the first time since he'd lost his memory, he hadn't had that nightmare.

He hadn't woken up covered in sweat and with

a devastating sense of loss. Hadn't felt a deeper question mark branded into his skin about that particular area of his past.

And it was because of Imogen.

Climbing onto the deck and striding to the small dining area where his wife sat, Zeph reaffirmed to himself that he'd made the right decision.

Ne, keeping Imogen around was the key to regaining his memories. And he wasn't going to let that opportunity slip through his fingers.

CHAPTER SEVEN

SHE'D LINGERED BENEATH the shower and relived every moment of the episode in the bedroom, alternating between kicking herself for letting things go so far and being disgruntled that somehow she'd once again ended up on the wrong side of Zeph when *he* bore the responsibility for her being here in the first place.

Then she'd forced herself to perform a ten-minute yoga session in her room to calm her racing mind. She'd left her cabin confident that she had her emotions under control.

Realistically, there was no way she could get out of the six months Zeph had demanded she spend with him. The 'I'll never forget' part was one she would have to play by ear. And she was most definitely not going to think about it now.

Sipping her coffee, she glanced at the place setting across from hers, telling herself she was prepared for whatever happened with Zeph.

Imogen knew all her calming efforts had failed the moment Zeph stepped onto the deck, brimming with male confidence, looking entirely too dashing in his all white attire—dear God, did any colour *not* look incredible on that body?—and making a beeline for her. Once again, he was barefoot, which made him, curiously, even more compelling. Like a man fundamentally connected to the cosmos and confident of his place in the world.

Against her will, she searched his face, her heart thumping wildly at the thought of everything that had happened between them. Wondered whether the icy condemnation he'd left her with still lingered.

When he merely pulled out a seat and sat down, she felt a little bit of wind ease from her sails, and took a tiny breath.

Once they'd been served coffee and fruit and he'd snapped his linen napkin loose, his gaze drifted over to her. She hated herself for her breath catching in her midriff, her senses on tenterhooks as she waited for him to speak.

'Is that get-up supposed to put me off?' he drawled, his gaze drifting over the long-sleeved blouse and pencil skirt she'd worn.

'Can we not do this, please?' she said, a little desperately. Had she chosen the outfit to bolster her confidence? Yes, she had.

There's nothing wrong with that, she assured herself.

His amusement vanished, his eyes narrowing on her face. 'Do what?' he queried silkily.

'This…you know what I mean. You're trying to get a rise out of me.'

A hint of a smile reappeared but it was all cynicism. 'You're dressed like you're heading for the
office. Only a day after your husband has returned. One would think you didn't want to spend
any time with me. Not the look we want to project, I don't think?'

'It is a work day and I don't remember agreeing to abandon all work on this…jaunt you want
to go on.'

She cringed inside at how callous that sounded.
But what other choice did she have? She was following the example he had set two years ago.
After last night and what happened this morning, straying from the path felt like the riskiest
thing she could do. If he thought her uncaring,
then so be it.

Midnight-blue eyes turned a little flinty and
she shivered from the change in them. Silence
reigned for another minute before he drained his
espresso cup and poured another. Then he helped
himself to several cuts of Iberian ham specially
cured for the yacht. Adding buttered bread and
condiments, he took a bite and chewed while staring at her.

He swallowed and nodded. 'Very well. If that's
how you want to play it.'

Her stomach knotted. 'What does that mean?'

'Nothing sinister, Imogen. If you want to work

today, then we will work. I look forward to shadowing you.'

She shook her head. 'You can't mean…'

'That's exactly what I mean. Now do you want to discuss your schedule or shall I just ring up my assistant and muddle my way through?'

She snorted under her breath before she could stop herself. 'You've never muddled your way through anything. Let's not pretend you'll do that now.'

His lips twitched. 'I hear a compliment in there somewhere. I think I'll take it.' With that he continued eating, his healthy appetite almost hypnotic to watch.

She forced herself to eat a few bites of food, ignoring his steady gaze on her plate and his frown when she pushed the half-eaten meal away.

Her mind was still whirling when he rose to his feet and, for the life of her, Imogen could not get the image of him, fully naked, commandingly aroused and in the throes of his pleasure, out of her mind.

And heaven help her, he saw her struggle, leaning down over her chair, and brushed his lips against her earlobe. 'I'm not going anywhere, dear wife. I suggest you get used to that very quickly.'

He sauntered out of the dining room, taking every ounce of air with him.

She told herself she rose and followed because

she wanted to get on with her day but there was an undeniable compulsion to see what Zeph would do next.

He reached the study before her but went to the window instead of taking the seat. Only after she had sat down and opened her laptop did he approach and take the seat next to her.

'What's first on the agenda?' he asked.

She clenched her gut against the hyperawareness his proximity triggered. 'I have to touch base with the board. We have a video conference starting in five minutes.'

He nodded, sat back and folded his arms.

She scrolled through a few emails, grimacing when she saw one that made her heart sink.

'Problem?' Zeph asked.

'The Canadian brothers are trying to throw spanners in the works.'

'Show me.'

Eyeing him for a moment, she turned the laptop so he could read the email. Astonishingly quickly, he'd read it and sat back. 'Ignore it.'

'What?'

'Let them stew for a bit. I find that focuses the mind. Five days, maybe a week should do it. Then tell them no. They take the deal on the table or we walk away.'

She opened her mouth to press him, ask if he

was sure. The loud beep of an incoming video call halted it.

'Trust me,' he murmured. 'And trust yourself.'

Imogen's eyes widened. Something jumped inside her. *Trust yourself.* It was more positive encouragement than she'd ever had in her life. And it scared her how much she wanted more. *Needed* it.

Grateful for the distraction, she pressed the button to the call and watched seven expressions fill the screen.

The oldest, Apostolos Goumas, the most out-spoken of the board members, glared fiercely at her.

From the very beginning, he'd disapproved of her, both as Zeph's chosen wife—a position ru-moured to be one he'd hoped his daughter would fill—and at her status on the board. No doubt he'd have discouraged his own daughter from taking up a space on the board he deemed should be re-served only for men.

'You have located your husband and you didn't see fit to inform us?' he barked.

Even from a few feet away she felt the burst of displeasure from Zeph. Probably because it was the same emotion threatening to burst free from her. Years of practice aided her in not blowing her top.

'First and foremost, I wasn't aware I answered

to you, Apostolos. Secondly, what would you have done had you known? If I recall, you've been urging me to have him declared lost at sea for several months now. So why the urgency to know he's alive and well?'

The old man bristled and leaned forward, no doubt to put Imogen in her place. But another board member interrupted before he could speak.

'Is he well?' Vasili asked.

In a pool of sharks, Vasili was perhaps the least aggressive. Not that he wasn't as prone to looking down his nose at her on occasion as his other colleagues. He just did it less.

She didn't need to glance across her desk to verify Zeph's well-being. She could feel his animal magnetism like a force field, pressing down on her. Hell-bent on dominating her. 'Yes, he's well.'

After several seconds, once they realised she wasn't going to elaborate, their expression ranged from mild irritation to outright anger.

'Listen here, girl,' Apostolos snapped again. 'You have no right to keep us in the dark. As members of his board, we need to know when he will return. *If* he will return. What is his state of mind? And we need to know where he's been all this time, at the very least. You can't just pick and choose when you—'

'He's my husband. I think you'll find I can.'

His face grew redder. 'What about the impact this news could have on the stock market? It could be catastrophic.'

'I checked it this morning, as I'm sure you did too, so you'll know it's doing very well. And I disagree. I think news of Zeph's return will be fantastic for Diamandis stock. But that won't be done according to your timetable, Apostolos. Or at the whim of anyone else on the board, for that matter.'

Several outraged expressions filled the screen at her.

Trust yourself.

She wanted to glance Zeph's way but she kept her gaze straight, her focus neutral.

Of course, Apostolos was the first to vocalise his affront. 'You dare to lecture us on matters of the company's health?'

'It's less of a lecture and more of a disagreement,' she replied smoothly.

'How do we even know there's truth in this sudden rumour? None of us had any idea there was a chance that he could be alive. How do we know you're not making this—?'

Apostolos's belligerence whittled away when Zeph rose from his chair, stepped close and his image filled the space behind her. When he went one better and lowered his head alongside hers, several gasps filled the screen.

'I'm going to pretend I didn't just hear you call my wife a liar,' he said with icy hauteur.

One by one, she watched them reel back in shock, then cower beneath Zeph's fierce glare.

Bursts of speech and hastily put-together smiles appeared one by one. Zeph silenced them with the simple but effective act of raising his hand.

'*Kalismera*, gentlemen. As you can see, I am alive and well, as my wife just told you. I will be in touch with you when I deem it right. In the meantime, you will show my wife the respect she deserves.' He paused and swung his gaze to Apostolos. 'And the next time I hear you speak to her in any manner less than respectfully, you will not appreciate the consequences. Any of you.'

She was about to reach out and end the call when Zeph held up his hand.

'One more thing. My wife and I will not be available for the next few weeks. As you can understand, we have a lot of catching up to do. Can I be reassured that you will step in and manage the day-to-day?' It was framed as a question, but Imogen and the board members knew it was not. It was a directive.

There was the barest amount of fidgeting before agreeable nods reflected across the screens.

'Good,' he said. 'There is a matter with the Canadians my wife will send an email about shortly. That will be the end of her working day until further notice. But she will expect a full report at the end of each day from each of you.'

Then, amid the torrent of English and Greek that belatedly welcomed him back, Zeph pressed a button to end the call.

He didn't move away in the silence that ensued. He stayed right next to her, his scent filling her senses, his presence overwhelming her. And those eyes she truly believed saw beneath her skin boring straight into her.

'You didn't need to do that,' she murmured.

'No,' he concurred easily. 'But it was either do that or fire every last one of them.'

Her gaze swung to his, astonishment weaving through her. 'But…you've known some of them for years.'

He shrugged. 'I don't care. I will not have you disrespected.'

You don't even know me! What about when you regain your memories and realise I'm the enemy?

Imogen wanted to yell those statements at him. To keep common sense at the forefront of her mind and heart. And yet, those simply uttered words were burrowing inside her, seeking and warming the vulnerable place where she'd yearned for affection and affirmation. Where she'd despaired that she would never be good enough.

In that moment, not a single cell in her body could deny the effect of Zeph's words on her. Giving her what no other person on earth had given her.

Respect. Recognition. Acceptance.

She swallowed the sudden lump in her throat and glanced up. The gaze that met and held hers steadily zapped something else inside her.

Was that connection-seeking?

Was that loneliness she spotted deep in his eyes?

No. It couldn't be. She was getting carried away. Forgetting the sort of man she was dealing with. Even without recognising a single member of the board, he'd got them to jump to his command. It was simply the effect he had on mere mortals.

And if that effect included getting her onside…

She watched him return to his seat. 'And what was that about taking several weeks off?'

He tugged on her seat until she'd turned sideways to face him, one eyebrow quirked at her. 'Are you going to take my head off for it?'

Belatedly, she tried to summon irritation or hurt at his high-handedness. 'You planned this all along, didn't you?'

'Not entirely. But I can't help but notice that you are bearing the lion's share of the work when the board is there for a reason. None of them looked like they are in Athens currently. Am I wrong?'

She bit the inside of her cheek. 'They took their annual holidays last week.'

'All of them. At the same time?'

She shrugged. 'Is it really work if I enjoy it?'

'If it takes away time from your newly returned husband? Yes, it is. And before you say it, you may be unwilling but it's decided.'

'Just like that?'

'You went to all the trouble to find me. Pardon me if I'm not going to turn my back on whatever it is that is going on here. So you can come clean with whatever else you're withholding from me or we can spend time together. I said you had until tonight but I'm happy for you to give me your answer now.'

And with that ball lobbed firmly in her court, Imogen felt the last of her freedom draining away. 'Jeopardise your health by feeding you information or spend time in your company. Those are my choices?'

That smile reappeared. 'There is a third option, but I won't risk you running away from me again should I mention it.'

Her face flamed and his smile turned into laughter. And wasn't it just the most insulting icing on the cake that every cell in her body seemed to scream in delight at that sound?

'Very well. I will curate my time accordingly, and give you the six months.'

Undisguised triumph leapt into his eyes. *'Eh-faristo, yineka mou,'* he rasped. He started to reach out.

Fearing another touch, another caress would be too much, Imogen cleared her throat. 'What do you want to do first?'

Without answering he rose and went to the yacht's intercom. She watched him press the button that connected him to the captain and proceed to have a conversation in Greek she didn't understand.

That done, he turned and strolled back towards her, the swagger in his walk wreaking utter havoc with her breathing.

'I've just asked the captain to plot a chart for a few destinations. First stop, Montenegro. I'm in the mood for an adventure.'

That was the first in the series of alarming surprises in store for her that day. Once she'd sent the required emails informing her assistant and senior staff of her intended vacation, she went downstairs to her cabin, intending to change into a swimsuit to join Zeph for a mid-morning swim.

Her walk-in closet was empty. Every scrap of her belongings was gone, down to the dental floss she'd used last night.

Marching into the master suite down the hall, she knocked and received a deep-voiced, half-amused summons.

'You had my things moved?' she demanded, unwilling to look at the bed she'd rolled around in only a handful of hours ago or—after one heart-stopping glance at him—the man who was wearing swim shorts and nothing else.

Of course, she caught his eloquent shrug from the corner of her eye. 'I anticipated your agreement and acted on it. You can choose to be affronted or chalk it up to expediency.'

'But we were…we had separate sleeping arrangements before.'

His nostrils pinched. 'Yes. *Before*. It doesn't work for me any more.'

'Why not? Because of appearances? You didn't care about what the staff thought before.'

Something lit at the back of his eyes, too impenetrable for her to work through, and it was gone before she could figure it out. 'A lot of things happened before that I'm seeking to alter.'

Her heart lurched. What did that mean? Imogen felt like ten kinds of coward for not being strong enough to insist on an elaboration. Not because she wasn't yearning to know, but because she was alarmed by the possibility that the answer he gave, if it wasn't the right one, might bruise her.

Her mouth worked, as if she'd love nothing better than to rip into him for his assumption. Something in Zeph's belly jumped, hot anticipation swirling through his veins. He was almost sorry when she waved a dismissive hand. Because a small part of him also wanted that interrogation, just so he could work his way through why he'd given the instruction. Yes, he wanted his wife in his bed. But he suspected it went beyond that. An intense, unfamiliar need knotted in his belly that had nothing to do with sex. That compelled him to act in a way that clearly—if his wife was to be believed—was unlike him.

And that need wouldn't be denied.

'I'll let it go, this once. Please don't make it a habit.' Her gaze, compelled by his unrelenting masculinity, skated over him again. 'And just so we're clear, we still won't be having sex.' Desperate words ripped from desperate senses that mocked her even as she said them. But she was proud of herself for drawing that line. Because stepping over it would be the last word in lunacy.

Wouldn't it?

He curbed a smile, wisely guessing it wouldn't be welcome. 'Understood, wife.'

Her nostrils pinched in a quick inhale. 'All this is one giant joke to you, isn't it?'

'Not at all. I just don't see the need to expend

energy on fighting when we could be using that energy efficiency elsewhere.'

'Like sex, you mean?' she threw at him. Or attempted to. She failed when her cheek flared bright red again and her eyes grew that stormy shade he'd come to associate with her arousal.

Oh, yes, his wife wanted him as much as he wanted her.

But not yet. 'Eventually,' he responded, much to the chagrin and disappointment of his raging libido.

Her widened gaze said his answer had thrown her too. She cast her gaze around, lingering on the bed before flitting away. 'Then…what do you have in mind?'

Zeph stifled a groan.

Theós, was he better off just getting the sex out of the way so they could breathe for a time without it clouding every thought?

He pushed the boulder of craving away. 'Believe it or not, I'd like to discuss you.'

Those alluring eyes grew wider. 'M-me?'

'No need to look so alarmed, *glikia mou*. It's just a conversation. Which we will have after you get out of that insultingly boring get-up.'

She made a noise that sounded very much like a snort of disbelief, dragging further humour to the surface.

As she sailed to the twin dressing room where

he'd had her things relocated with her pert little nose in the air, Zeph wandered to the balcony.

He'd noted how his occasional smile had drawn surprise from his crew. How his board members, even though every one of them deserved his ire for the way they'd treated Imogen, had all jumped at his appearance.

Was he a humourless bastard on top of everything else? Was that part of the reason Imogen tried to hold him at arm's length?

With a grunt he pushed *that* too away.

Imogen had already given away more than he knew she'd intended to. He just needed to be patient and not push her too far too soon. What he wanted would come to him soon enough. Even if the torture of it might feel unbearable at times.

Like this morning...

He clenched his belly against the punch of hunger and turned around.

And almost swallowed his tongue when she walked out of the dressing room wearing a gold bikini moulded onto her skin.

He'd seen how beautiful she was this morning when she'd writhed beneath him. But as he gained some distance now, taking in the whole package, Zeph's breath was knocked clean out of his lungs by his wife's breathtaking beauty.

Theós, I'm never going to let her go.

He shook himself free of that visceral declaration that lit up in him. Shook himself free of the unnerving tenacity of it. He'd laid out his terms. She'd agreed to them.

It might not even come to that. He might be cured of this...*need* long before then.

He ignored the sceptical voice that trailed in his head as he crossed the room to her. He sensed her nervousness as she walked beside him to the open aft lounging area past the sprawling swimming pool on Deck Two.

Choosing twin loungers, he dropped into one and watched her set her back down and generally fidget while avoiding his gaze.

'Relax, Imogen.'

'Easier said than done,' she returned, her full mouth set into a displeased line.

'When was the last time you had a holiday?'

She shrugged. 'I don't recall.'

'You don't recall? I'm the one with the memory issues. If you don't recall then this one is long overdue.'

Now, she glanced his way, and that jumpiness in his belly lessened. 'You should talk. I have it on good authority from your PA that you'd never taken a vacation in almost a decade before you... went missing.'

When he raised his eyebrows at her, she elaborated.

'It was part of trying to find you. Spyros has

been your assistant for eight years. He said the
only time you used the yacht or any of your
homes around the world was if you were attend-
ing a business meeting or hosting whatever fun-
draising gala you were patron of. He also said
you have a pathological dislike of hotel rooms,
hence the insane amount of properties you own.'

'Is one of those in Lake Como?' he asked without any clear idea why the location slipped from
his lips.

She nodded, her eyes widening on his. 'Yes.
Does it ring a bell?' she asked, her voice pitched
with expectation. Or was it alarm?

He slotted that information away as he
shrugged. 'I'm not sure. It just jumped into my
head.'

Her pink tongue darted out to lick her lips, and
he had to clench his gut again—a frustratingly
frequent occurrence around this woman. 'Well,
you have a beautiful property right on the edge
of the lake.'

'I look forward to revisiting it, then. Seeing if
it triggers anything.'

Even though she nodded, that wary look lingered in her eyes.

Back on Efemia, he probably would've taken
pity on anyone so skittish around him—not that
there had been many. But he couldn't seem to
control his impulses around Imogen.

He stretched out on the lounger, aware that she'd grown even tenser. 'You were going to tell me all about yourself.'

'No, you were demanding that I do. I hadn't quite agreed.'

He sighed. 'Is this to be another bone of contention? I'm beginning to think you like arguing with me for the sake of it.'

A startled look widened her eyes, triggering the sense that he'd just scored a bullseye. After gliding on sun protection in quick motions, she set the bottle aside and cleared her throat. 'Shall I summarise my life for you?' she asked, then continued before he could respond. 'I'm an only child. My father wanted a son but got me instead.'

The words were clipped, but Zeph heard the unspoken turmoil wrapped around them.

'We never really...clicked. I spent more time with my nannies than with Dad when I was growing up.'

'And your mother? Where was she in all this?'

After a brief hesitation, she said, 'She died a few weeks after I was born. Complication of birth, I was told.'

He muttered a response then realised he'd spoken Greek. Before he could translate, she offered a smile and a nod.

Zeph's gaze fell on the monogrammed towel nearby, the extravagant 'O' followed by the letters that spelled out the name of a mother he couldn't remember. Was he foolish to feel a kinship with Imogen over an occurrence that affected millions? He realised his fingers were tracing the 'O' when she looked down and then up at him.

'Did I share details of my mother with you?'

Her face softened, even as she shook her head. 'No.'

Another disquieting feeling swelled within him. Just what had they shared?

Ask her. Or was he hesitant to know because of what it might mean? That, for whatever reason, it seemed he'd plucked a near stranger from Texas and married her to suit his own ends?

A little annoyed with the deluge of internal questions and demands tumbling around inside him, he pushed ahead.

'Where is your father? What is he doing now?'

Again those pinched lips that spelled her unhappiness about the subject. 'He's a consultant for my cousin's oil company in Texas.'

'I'm surprised he's not here attempting to help you run a multibillion-euro company. It seems like that's the kind of thing a man who wishes for a son instead of a daughter would jump at the opportunity to do.' At her lengthy silence, his eyes narrowed shrewdly on her. 'He tried, didn't he?'

She nodded. 'A few months after you went missing, he came to Athens. Offered to help me run the ship until you were found. I, and the board, disagreed.'

Zeph pursed his lips, his impression of the men he'd spoken with this morning only marginally improving. 'Glad to know they're good for something, although I think they were guarding their own interests rather than looking out for yours. And I'm guessing when you refused, your father didn't stay to offer his support anyway?'

Imogen wondered whether he knew there was bitterness bleeding through his voice; whether his acrimonious feelings for her family were subconsciously slipping through the blank fog of his memories to manifest impressions he didn't know about.

'No, he didn't. He gave his unsought opinion on my competency and left. We haven't spoken that much since then.'

After several moments, layers of that acidity still lingered. She startled when the back of his hand brushed hers. 'You stood up to him, protected what was important to you. Very little else matters.'

She wanted to laugh. Because on the one hand it sounded like much-desired praise. But on the other, it was exactly what he'd done to her to ensure her and her father's capitulation. He'd leveraged her to ruin her family.

She shook her head, ruthlessly pushing back

the tumult his questions had brought. 'That's me in a nutshell.' Before he could probe deeper, she rose and approached the pool. This deck was level with the sea, the extended diving platform the perfect place for launching into the glittering waters of the Aegean.

And that was exactly what she did.

Zeph watched her execute a perfect dive into the sea, his breath uselessly shortened by the impact of her stunning body. Surfacing several dozen feet away, she cut lazily through the water before flipping to float on her back.

After watching her for several minutes, and attempting to resist the impossible, he did what he'd been doing since he walked onto his yacht.

He rose and went after his wife.

Imogen didn't need to look to know when Zeph entered the water. She was beginning to fear this hyperawareness would become fused into her psyche. Hell, she was living in a state of mild panic about everything to do with her husband.

That realisation was what had sent her into the sea instead of the swimming pool. The need to lose herself in something bigger than herself. Than Zeph.

If that was even possible.

The sea…

She jerked up from her floating, her gaze searching for Zeph. Although his strokes were powerful and confident, her heart continued to beat wildly as he cut through the water towards her.

When he reached her, she blurted, 'I'm sorry, I didn't think…'

Another stroke brought him within touching distance.

His legs tangled with hers beneath the waters, effortlessly keeping them both afloat. 'Calm yourself. I don't see the sea as a place of trauma. It had a chance to take me. It didn't.' His lips quirked. 'I returned to it as a fisherman for the better part of a year.'

Imogen snorted, then smiled. 'I'm still wrapping my head around that. The billionaire turned fisherman, hauling his daily catch to make a living.'

His teeth flashed, highlighting his chiselled perfection. 'A feast for the tabloids should it come out, I think.'

'There's no doubt it's going to come out. I was forced to announce who you were in a church full of people, remember? It's only a matter of when it comes out.'

'We'll handle it when the time comes.'

She nodded, her insides melting at the sound of the 'we'. They bobbed around in the water for another minute before she glanced up at him.

'Did you enjoy it? Were you…happy?' she murmured.

His expression was contemplative for a minute before he answered. 'I had nothing else to compare it to, so I made the most of it.'

A more practical answer than she'd anticipated. And yet, it was exactly the kind the old Zeph and perhaps even this new Zeph epitomised. Taking the raw ingredients handed to them by life or circumstances and turning them into something invaluable.

Wasn't that what he'd done after the horrific destitution brought on by the Callahans? Zeph Diamandis, at the tender age of nineteen, had turned his family's fortunes around. Built a global empire out of the ashes of acrimony.

'But there were always questions. Beyond my missing memories.'

Her gaze sharpened on his face, her heart dancing around in her chest at the seriousness of his expression. 'Questions?'

He shrugged. 'I'm no neurological expert but a grown man having recurring dreams about a childhood version of himself in distress definitely raises a few questions, *ochi*?'

Imogen strove to keep her feelings from showing. To keep herself from tensing within his arms. And it took everything she had to execute a small, understanding nod.

While her heart dropped into her stomach at the knowledge that once he regained his memories, Zeph would surely damn her for keeping this from him.

CHAPTER EIGHT

THAT ATE AT her for the next two weeks.

Weeks during which they explored their way up and down the Mediterranean and Adriatic seas. Where they visited four of his homes and she watched him take pleasure in such simple things as manning a barbecue on the terrace of his mansion in St Tropez or drinking a beer on a beach in Montenegro while watching the sunset.

Of course, they took time out of their day to take care of pressing business. It started with Imogen calling a meeting of their high-echelon staff and his press office.

'Forgive me if I don't remember names,' Zeph said without elaborating why he didn't. 'But I'm back and I wanted you all to see me since the rumours are swirling around.'

She watched as their eyes widened and they discreetly exchanged looks before they surrendered their attention to their boss.

He turned to his communications director. 'Send out a press release stating I'm back. My absence was caused by a moderate accident from which I'm still recovering. For now, I'm spending time with my wife and will return to the helm of my company in due course.'

The director cleared his throat. 'The financial world will be desperate to know specifics, Mr Diamandis.'

Zeph sent him a tight smile. 'That's what I employ you to handle. Tell them my wife has been in charge and will continue to be so for now until further notice. Nothing more than that.'

After that, Imogen got a kick out of watching the Canadian brothers grovel when she threatened to walk away from the deal, then watching them almost beg when Zeph backed up that threat.

They celebrated when the deal was done and dusted the very next day.

But Imogen remained in a state of flux, swinging between stunned surprise at the sometimes disarming charm Zeph exuded and awe at his continued astuteness when they were inevitably pulled into business matters. Those times she completely understood why he was at the top of his game in the business world. And to do it while not recalling any of the actual intricacies of the dealing? Imogen silently shook her head in wonder after the fourth time he skilfully negotiated another tricky transaction.

And then there were those gut-clenching, heart-racing times when he looked at her quizzically, as if trying to work out what she was keeping from him. Trying to work out *why* she was keeping it from him.

As for his amnesia, whether it was muscle memory or something else, small cracks were beginning to appear in the armour shrouding his memories.

Although infrequent, they were clustered in furtive bursts that the doctor said were not uncommon, projecting the possibility that his stagnant memory loss might be changing. For instance, last week Imogen had watched him dial his PA's number without referring to his contact information. The same PA whose last name Zeph couldn't remember.

To say that it kept Imogen on her toes was an understatement.

As for the sizzling attraction between them…

For whatever reason, Zeph had stopped pushing further after that morning in his stateroom. Imogen continually berated herself for the disappointed ache in her belly and the lustful need that kept her awake long after Zeph had fallen asleep beside her.

It wasn't a huge stretch to get that it stemmed from those frequent head massages she gave him to ease his headaches, and the proximity of just sharing a bed with her husband that kept her craving on max.

She told herself it was a good thing they had only gone so far and then it too began to sound hollow.

As had become a frequent thing, she was alternately berating and convincing herself about the pros when she walked into the smallest living room on the yacht and stopped dead.

Zeph was sitting on the futon-like cushion, a fierce competitive gleam in his eyes and his focus rapier sharp. Beside him sat Nike, their youngest crew member, equally engrossed in the activity. And that activity was what made her jaw sag to the floor.

Her husband was playing a video game!

For a full minute, they remained oblivious to her presence, a child-like engrossment in their activity making her lips twitch.

But if she'd thought Zeph would remain oblivious for long, she was mistaken. Without glancing her way, he said, 'Once again, I seem to have shocked you, wife.'

'I...yes, I admit you have.'

Pausing the game, he glanced at the young steward and, heeding the silent command, the boy scrambled up and left the room.

Zephyr waved to the vacated seat and Immie found herself accepting the invitation. Still stunned, she ambled over the armchair and sank into it. Her shock grew when he held out the controller.

'What? You want me to play with you?'

His head tilted fractionally and her breath

caught, sensing that while he looked outwardly relaxed, that labyrinthine brain had gone into full calculus mode.

'I do. But, unlike with young Nike, I wish to make ours more interesting.'

Oh, God.

She should refuse now, even before he spelled out what he meant. She was dealing with a master negotiator. One who'd brokered one of the world's most complicated deals. Wall Street still spoke with the awe of the Diamandis-Avalon deal most called the deal of the century.

'I'm not playing some sketchy version of video-game strip poker with you, if that's what you're angling for.'

His gaze heated, his smile devastating. 'Why, what a dirty mind you have.'

Heat rushed into her face, and he gave a low laugh. 'What do you have in mind, then?'

'A party for my thirty-fifth,' he announced immediately. 'At the Lake Como residence when we get there next week.'

Her eyes widened, then she frowned. 'You don't need to compete with me in order to throw a party. It's your birthday. And your property. You can do whatever you want.' And because every small reference to his memory loss brought brooding displeasure and she wanted to keep this atmosphere light, she refrained from pointing out the possible adverse effect of throwing a party for guests, most of whom he wouldn't recognise.

He turned and faced her fully. 'All true. But I find things work smoother for me when your wholehearted endorsement is involved.'

Please. Please...don't.

But it was too late. Her heart was doing that leaping, exhilarated, roller-coaster-ride thing that made her dizzy. Made her want to shake her head to establish rational thinking.

She was still reeling from his words when he reached out, tucked a strand of hair behind her ear, and waved the controller at her once more. *'Ne?'*

And that was how she found herself playing a video game with Zephyr Diamandis.

Naturally, he trounced her because his dominating, competitive spirit wouldn't allow for anything else.

And by that afternoon, she was instructing caterers, event planners and liaising with her and Zeph's PAs to put together a guest list that very quickly risked growing into over a thousand.

She was wondering whether it was wise to broach the subject of exposing himself to so many people at once a few days later when he leaned across the table in the restaurant they'd come to for dinner after docking on the shores of the historic and stunning Hvar on the Croatian coast.

The single candle threw shadows across his breathtaking face as he levelled a stare at her. 'Dance with me,' he rasped, holding out his hand.

She started, looked around her, ready to point out there was no dance floor. But indeed, there was one. A small mosaic-tiled floor tucked away into one corner of the restaurant. Currently an older couple were the only occupants on the dance floor, swaying gently to the low but beautifully stirring music.

'I...'

His nostrils flared at her slight hesitation but a moment later, the flicker of displeasure disappeared from his eyes. 'Call it an exploratory mission, if you must. I'd rather not discover that I can't dance at my party.'

'We both know inadequacy of any kind isn't in your vocabulary.'

'Then let's confirm it, shall we?'

With that neat counter, she had very little else to sustain the argument besides an outright *no*. And Imogen...didn't want to.

She placed her hand in his and let him lead her to the dance floor. Let him draw her into his arms and wrap one arm around her waist.

She swayed, breathing him in, his intoxicating male scent making her stifle a groan.

It was the first time they'd shared a sustained closeness for weeks. Yes, the massages she gave him to ease his headaches required close contact but, more often than not, he succumbed to sleep within five minutes, leaving her oddly satisfied and uplifted, and yet empty.

Something in her leapt in delight and then settled in contentment as they swayed in silence, one slow and rhythmic song blending into another. By the third, her insides were melting again, as they seemed to do around him. Imogen clung shamelessly to him, and when he wrapped both arms around her waist, she stifled a low moan.

The evening was coming to a close but she didn't want this to end. She—

'How long are you going to torture us both, Imogen?'

She jerked against him in surprise, rearing back from where she had tucked her face into his neck. 'What do you mean?'

His face tightened, the barest hint of a grimace crossing his expression before disappearing. 'I mean how long do I have to endure lying next to you, night after night, unable to touch you?'

Her eyes widened. 'But you...you fall asleep before I do most nights.'

A wry smile twisted his lips. 'I have become a master at that act. I pretend to be asleep so we don't both get agitated by unfulfilled needs.'

Her mouth gaped. 'No...'

'Yes,' he insisted firmly. 'So I ask again.

How long will this torment continue? I want you, Imogen.'

Her heart leapt, then danced wildly. Still she tried to contain it. 'Zeph, I don't think…'

His lips firmed. 'Of course you don't. You would rather deny what you truly want than give in to me. Is that it?'

That was exactly it.

And yet in that moment it felt like a battle that didn't need to be fought. She was a starving woman fighting not to take a morsel off the veritable feast at her disposal.

How long was she going to sustain this hunger? When every argument she had put up felt like an exercise in unnecessary self-flagellation?

So what if she was the one who had stipulated the no sex between them? He'd honoured her request, had turned down the seduction dial, which had adversely maddened her of late. But that time had been enough to know, whatever his agenda was, it wasn't to overwhelm her with sex. Or the promise of it. But if he was as tortured as she'd become lately…

Could she change her mind again now? Why not? She was a grown woman. Did she not have the right to change her mind? Especially if it was what they both wanted?

The voice of caution started to rise but he was still swaying them across the dance floor, maintaining an iron will on his control despite those hypnotic eyes coaxing her into sin. And with every minute that passed, she yearned harder to sink into the passionate chaos, to get a true taste of what it felt like to lose herself in the promise in his eyes.

Would she regret it at some point in the very near future? Possibly. But it was a mistake she was willing to confront when the time came.

And what if it grows past a mistake? What if you risk everything?

She wouldn't, she promised herself.

'Such a lengthy debate,' he mused, but the clench of his face told her that he was anticipating her answer perhaps even more than she. Was gearing up to put up a fight if need be. 'Do you have the balls to vocalise it so I might advocate for myself? Because I cannot take another night of torment.'

And the fact that he wanted her this much was a lit match held against the touchpaper of her desires. So when he swayed them for another handful of seconds and then growled, 'Imogen,' she knew there was only one answer to give.

'Yes.'

His stare intensified, devouring her alive. 'Yes, to what, exactly, *eros mou*?'

'Yes, to whatever you want.'

His nostrils flared, and the light of triumph in

his eyes turned them almost incandescent. Every cell in her body jerked to life, the promise in his gaze almost too much to bear. She gave the tiniest whimper when he stepped away but in the next breath he was taking her hand, tugging her off the dance floor.

'Come,' he commanded.

He nodded at the security that had become necessary after news of Zeph's return had hit the world media. As predicted, the stocks had soared, the politely contrite board members delighted by their unexpected windfall. Speculation had been rife, prompting them to issue a press release stating the barest of facts and withholding the fact that Zeph Diamandis was suffering from amnesia. As far as he was concerned, it was nobody's business but theirs.

His request for privacy hadn't been heeded, of course, meaning that they were stealthier about when they came ashore. Like tonight.

The man spoke into a walkie-talkie and a minute later the luxury sedan was whisking them away, back to the yacht.

The moment they stepped aboard, Zeph swept her into his arms.

Surprised laughter left her throat. 'It'd be much faster if I were to walk, you know?'

He looked down at her for a moment, then brushed his lips briefly over hers. 'But then I wouldn't have you close. And I need that, *eros mou*. I've needed that for far longer than is acceptable.'

The arrogance in those words wasn't surprising. Hell, they triggered equal need in her so that by the time they arrived in their stateroom and he set her down on her feet, she was hopelessly damp between her legs and her chest rose and fell in pants that had his eyes darkening as they dropped to her chest.

The orange wraparound dress she wore came free under his urgent ministrations.

His eyes riveted on hers, Zeph tugged the flimsy cotton off her shoulders and tossed it away. And then his eyes dropped, his breath coming out raggedly when he took in the burnt-orange lace underwear shielding her nakedness.

'*Christos*, you are breathtaking.'

A pulse of feminine power sent her shoulders back, arousal dripping deliciously through her as she displayed herself for him. Between one breath and the next, he dropped to his knees, his hands clasping her hips.

Boldly he leaned forward and pressed his mouth to the apex of her thighs, his nostrils flaring as he decadently breathed her in.

Imogen gasped, her hands sinking into his hair to stop from toppling over. The brazenness of his arousal was both shocking and intoxicating.

She was absorbing these new, thrilling sensations when he sank his fingers into the delicate lace and ripped it off her body. Her louder gasp earned her a feral smile.

'Forgive me,' he said.

She laughed. 'Somehow I don't think you truly mean that.'

He shrugged. 'I will buy you a dozen more.'

'I can buy them for myself, thank you. But bear in mind that what goes around comes around.'

His eyes gleamed with something resembling respect.

In the next breath though, his expression was changing, his gaze dropping to the place he had uncovered. He muttered something in Greek she didn't quite catch, and then he was lifting her leg, throwing it over his shoulder and pressing his mouth to her heated core.

Imogen yelped, delight overtaking her instantly. 'Zeph!'

Her shout out of his name accompanied the crumbling of her knees. He caught her easily, splaying her out on the carpet like a sumptuous feast before delving back between her thighs.

Her back arched, her senses flowering wide open as desire overtook her.

Perhaps it was because so much time had passed since the first time he'd done this to her, but Imogen felt every stroke of his tongue with twice the delight. Twice the saturated pleasure. And in no time at all, she was thrown into a sweet and turbulent climax, convulsions seizing her as she screamed his name.

She was coming down from the most exhilarating high of her life when she felt him tug off her bra.

He didn't immediately caress her breasts the way she had been expecting, instead his mouth trailed up her neck to her ear.

'I look forward to doing that again and again. And again. You look sublime when you are in the throes of passion,' he murmured.

She dragged her eyes open and stared into his heated ones.

His smile was laden with intent, his hands busy moulding her breasts now she had stopped panting. His gaze dropped to the tight nubs, watching his fingers torment her. When her fever started to rise again, Zeph paused.

Surging upright, he quickly discarded his clothes.

With one quick move, he scooped her up from the carpet and strode to the bed.

There, he perched her on the edge, sank fingers into her hair and sealed his mouth on hers in a kiss that had her blood singing wildly in her veins.

Imogen feared she was about to die of pleasure before he broke the kiss. With urgency that spoke of his waning control, Zeph retrieved a condom from the bedside table. With equally hurried movements, he sheathed himself and then reached for her.

Another ravishing kiss and he was bearing them down onto the bed. Finally he was wrapping those magic lips on one nipple, licking and sucking until her eyes rolled. Until all rational thought dissolved.

'Please, Zeph. Please!'

Firm hands gripped her thighs, spread her wide and then he straightened, staring down at her for a minute before he notched his rigid length against her core.

With one relentless thrust, he was surging deep, deeper inside her. Her eyes rolled shut as bliss overtook her, her legs rising to circle his hips in a desperate need to keep him right there.

'Open your eyes, Imogen. Watch me. Be reminded of who you belong to.'

She opened them, met his gaze again. 'You think I've forgotten? That I can ever forget?' There was a trace of lamentation in her heart when she said those words. Because it dawned on her that, whatever happened, she would never get through a day without thinking of him. Whether he heard it or not, the only visible response was primal. A flare of possessiveness in his eyes that accepted her words as his due.

'Poly kalos.' Very good. 'But you will watch all the same. Because I think we've established that it is better this way, *ochi*?'

God. This dogged determination. This raw, carnal demand from a man who'd plucked her from Texas, slapped his name on her then pretended she didn't exist? It was slicing away her fortitude layer by layer. And Imogen was terrified of what he might eventually uncover—a hungry, yearning soul, desperate for warmth. For love?

One hand slipped beneath her shoulder blades to clench in her hair as the other gripped her hip. And then he was pounding into her, every look, every touch, every caress denied until now feeding a ravenous hunger that demanded fulfilment.

When she thought she would go clean out of her mind, when she believed that there would be nothing left by the time he was done with her, another layer of pleasure sent her soaring off the peak, one scream piling into another in a blinding climax.

Above her, Zeph kept her pinned under his gaze and under his hold as he chased his own bliss. Thick words of Greek poured from him, his colour rising as the tempo intensified.

'You were worth the wait, *eros mou*.'

And with that, he threw his head back and

roared his release, the sensation so incredible, it triggered a fresh climax in her.

Together they shattered again and again until they were boneless, consisting only of jagged breaths and sweaty skin. Somehow, they made it onto the centre of the bed. She curled her arms around a pillow as Zeph strode to the bathroom to dispose of the condom. She was drifting off by the time he returned.

'We need to shower,' she slurred.

'In a while. Come here.' He pulled her in his arms and Imogen gave up and let herself melt into him.

He had bargained his way into the most sublime experience of his life.

When it became clear that growled commands and charmed proximity weren't going to work, Zeph had decided on the next best options. Retreat. Patience.

As much as it had tortured him to keep his hands off her, he had had the opportunity to learn new things about his wife. Impressive things.

And heaven help him if that hadn't made her even more alluring to him. He hadn't lied when he had said the past few weeks had been torture. And now, with sweat still slicking his body and hers, he should've felt the satisfaction of conquest. The satiation of his hunger.

He felt neither of those things.

All he felt was the clamour for more.

More of everything.

That hollowness within him that had been part of him for the past ten months was still as empty now as it was the morning Imogen had found him. But this time, he suspected he knew the answer to this peculiar hunger. Or was he merely clutching at straws?

Was he accepting what was right in front of him as the only option? Did he truly fear what else was out there?

No. He didn't. What he feared, though, was that this ache might never ease.

His hands tightened on her when she squirmed in her sleep. And just like that, his need rose again. Perhaps not even for sex.

I'm never going to let her go.

Stronger, more determined, those words filled his head until he half wished for the distraction of one of his headaches. He snorted under his breath. Even that had been taken care of by the woman in his arms.

Was that why he was overblowing her position in his life?

Questions teemed until he let out a low growl of frustration.

They were heading to Lake Como. After his party, they would return to Athens. Perhaps back in the real world, this reliance on Imogen would dissipate.

And if it doesn't?

He pushed the voice away, dropped a kiss on her temple and permitted sleep to lure him away too.

'You owe me a pleasuring, *eros mou*,' he rasped in her ear, right before his teeth nipped her lobe.

Imogen met his gaze over her shoulder, her breath emerging in tiny gasps. She'd woken ten minutes ago and attempted to sneak off to take a shower. She hadn't been surprised when Zeph had followed less than a minute later. 'And you want to collect now?'

'Oh, yes. I can't think of a better time than now.'

Sheer decadent delight pulsed through her as she turned and slowly sank onto her knees. The sight she made must have thrilled him because his manhood surged up from half-mast to full, his lips parting as his dark eyes sizzled on her.

Slowly, she dragged her hands up over his calves, over thickly muscled thighs that bunched and flexed under her touch. By the time she reached the shaft jutting proudly from its silky nest, they were both panting.

Just like before, Zeph watched her every

move, his head bent and hands braced on the marble wall.

Imogen took hold of him, her wet palm gliding over his rigid, veined flesh. A sizzling hiss erupted from him, and his thighs bunched as he fought for control.

Hot, heady power spiralled through her, the knowledge that even on her knees she could reduce him to such need triggering her own craving for this man.

But behind that power was a flare of panic. That she would want this a little too much to walk away from and return to their strained existence when their six months was up. That if she wasn't careful too much yearning might wreck her beyond salvaging.

His thick groan echoed in the heated space and she allowed it to sweep those thoughts away. Pulling him deeper into her mouth, she laved him with her tongue, suckled him so thoroughly it drew a torrent of filthy words from his mouth.

And all through it, she watched him as he watched her, because that connection they seemed to find so easily was a heady addition she was growing addicted to.

And when the Greek god of the man who looked even more devastatingly beautiful beneath the torrent of water reached his climax and bellowed it without reserve, Imogen sensed she was on the precipice of a potential life-altering event.

Protect yourself. Now.

She would have to find the strength to step away. Had she been able to resist the gentle hands that drew her to her feet. The mouth that anointed hers with soft but firm, claiming kisses. The body that braced hers as he washed her from head to foot, dried her body, then swept her off her feet, carrying her into the bedroom and into their bed, before drawing soft sheets over her body.

She couldn't have stopped herself from going into his arms right then if her life depended on it. So she didn't bother to resist.

And when he woke in the night with another nightmare and she was done soothing him, she let him cling tightly to her, her heart aching for everything she couldn't have. And the vital answer she was denying him.

Addicted.

Zeph was addicted to his wife. He'd searched for other words but kept alighting back on this one. Perhaps he'd sensed this was coming in that church when she'd stalked in on high heels and defiance to reclaim him. Perhaps that was why he'd made her jump through hoops before leaving with her.

Because now he was fighting a battle he was

sure he would lose. A battle he wasn't fully certain he *even wanted* to fight. And that in itself was alarming. Because despite his lost memories, at every step in the past ten months he'd been sure of his every move. He either was for or against a decision. Either in or out.

But now…

He felt unstitched. Picked apart. As if his favourite clothes no longer fitted. Scratched and chafed. Uncomfortable. And yet he had nothing to replace it with. He was rummaging in the dark and coming up empty. Because someone else held the key to refitting him?

Imogen?

No. Only he held the key to his destiny. Didn't he?

His heart thudded at the uncertainty that continued to flail inside him. It had expanded after they'd made love for the first time. And he couldn't find anything to shore it.

Hoping to alleviate it by sheer willpower, he kept his gaze on the house rising from the cliffs on the horizon.

The property in Lake Como.

The one he'd felt drawn to since they'd started this journey. If he didn't find answers there… then what?

Could he trust the strong urges that said Imogen was his key? And what if she left—?

Slim arms wound around his waist from behind, stalling his thoughts.

His heart leapt, even as dismay swelled like the waves rising against the hull of the yacht.

'There you are. Everything all right?'

Was that trepidation in her voice or was he projecting? He wanted to turn around, make sure but, shockingly, he was reluctant to confirm. And still that chafing continued. Persistent. Harder.

'Why shouldn't it be?' That emerged sharper than he'd intended, and he was unprepared for the deep flinch inside.

Imogen stiffened slightly, then, as he'd come to witness, she rallied. Far too effectively.

Really? Was he now jealous of his wife's ability to bounce back from his thoughtlessness? He was inwardly shaking his head when she continued.

'Everything is ready for the party tomorrow night,' she said, still tucked up behind him, her head on his shoulder.

He nodded, eyes narrowed on their destination, willing something…*anything* to kick him out of his mental fog. At least then he could make definitive decisions.

Like whether to redouble his efforts to keep his wife?

'Zeph?'

He shook himself free of all thought and focused on what she'd said. *'Efharisto.'*

'You don't need to thank me. I barely did anything. A handful of calls and everyone was doing backflips to host Zeph Diamandis's party. Hell, I think they would've probably done it for free for the bragging rights alone.' There was amusement in her voice and when he pulled his gaze from the mansion that so far offered no answers and looked down at her, she was smiling.

A bright, blindingly beautiful smile that made his heart leap. Again.

Theós, whatever this was, he had it bad.

He stared at her until she gave the tiniest squirm. Had he not known her as intimately as he did, he would've missed it.

'Zeph?' She searched his face, concern creasing her forehead. 'If you're not sure about the party, we can always cancel?'

That chafing intensified. 'Is that what you want? For me to cancel it?'

She hesitated, licking her lower lip before she answered. 'I know it's your birthday, but maybe it doesn't have to be on such a grand scale?'

'Yes, it does. I'm done hiding away, *yineka mou*. After the party, we're returning to Athens.'

This time he felt the full effect of her stiffening. 'We are? I thought you wanted six months.'

'I still do, but the remainder of the time won't be spent on the yacht.'

'But what about your…memory loss?'

That aching loss swelled but he pushed it down. 'If I have to live with it for longer than I want, then so be it. Do you doubt that I can cope? Is that why you're nervous?' he probed.

Her smile wasn't as brilliant as before when she answered with a forced laugh. 'Not at all. The last thing I'd doubt is your ability to do exactly as you please.'

The trace of acerbity was unmistakeable. But he couldn't do anything about it because the head steward was striding towards them, informing them they were about to dock.

And at the top of the stone stairs leading to the house, a line of staff waited to greet them.

Introductions brought no sudden enlightenment. No sudden lifting of the veil. He refused a tour of the house when it became clear the event planners were in full flow, readying the mansion for the party.

Instead, he demanded directions to his master suite, and when he had them, he took hold of his wife's hand.

'Where are we going?' she asked.

And, oh, what her husky voice did to his insides. How he wanted to drown in her until all the loud emptiness stopped tolling its presence.

'I know what I want to do before the madness starts,' he rasped against her lips when he reached the bottom of the grand staircase.

'What?'

'You have one guess, *yineka mou*.'

A delightful blush stained her cheeks and her breathing grew agitated, just the way he liked it.

Ne, he was addicted. And he feared it was a condition he wouldn't be free of any time soon.

The sex had helped.

But it didn't remove the hollow ache. If anything it had exposed it to harsher light.

Zeph acknowledged that as he buttoned his black silk shirt the next evening in preparation for the party.

Across the room in the adjoining dressing room, Imogen was getting dressed. His fingers slowed and he listened to the sounds of her getting ready. Zeph knew deep in his bones he'd never done anything of the sort before. And yet, he stilled, recognising the steadfast desire that this was what he wanted. For as long as he could keep it.

No force. No cajoling. No negotiation.

There was no such thing as a free lunch, as the saying went. But surely there was such a thing as simply…exposing one's wants and desires with the expectation that they would be reciprocated?

Bold. Daring. A shot entirely plausible for the man the world believed him to be to aim for.

But what about the man he was inside? Did he

dare expose himself thus? Take a risk with no surety of a reward?

Ne.

The affirmation was deep. Visceral.

And it immobilised him for endless moments until the sound of Imogen's footsteps roused him. He turned and then swayed on his feet at the sight of her.

The black, strapless velvet hugged her chest to hip and the scalloped plunging neckline decorated with sparkling crystals emphasised her assets tastefully but with jaw-dropping effect. 'You look exquisite, *matia mou*,' he croaked.

Her lashes swept down and a blush rose in her cheeks. It still gave him a kick how she could hold her own among curmudgeonly men and bully frat boys masquerading as Canadian businessmen and yet blush so innocently at a compliment.

Now he'd made the decision, the need to push it, know where he stood was yet another ache intensified inside, demanding to be soothed.

But the sound of arriving boats and helicopters demanded their attention. And he also needed to get dressed. So he reluctantly slotted it onto the back burner, along with that faint tingle at the back of his mind that prodded him that he was forgetting something. Adding that to the pile of things to be tackled later, he finished buttoning his shirt.

'I have something for you.'

He went to the far side of the room where the safe was tucked behind a secret panel in the wall.

'You do? But it's your birthday. I should be giving you presents…'

As he raised his hand to the combination his gaze fell on his ring, his heart hammering harder. 'You've done enough. But if you want to gift me with something, you will get the opportunity to in due course.'

Her eyes widened. 'Cryptic much? I don't think I can stand the suspense.'

'You'll have to. Our guests are arriving.'

Without second thought, he keyed in the combination.

Imogen gasped as the lock sprang free. 'You just…did you know the combination beforehand?'

A little shaken, he shook his head. 'No, I did not.'

They stared at one another for several more beats, then he opened the safe, extracted the long jewellery box he'd had Spyros courier from Athens before their arrival.

The necklace was a simple platinum chain but the teardrop diamond that hung from it was exceptional. Multifaceted to catch the light from every angle, it sparkled as he held it out to her.

Shock widened her eyes, confirming his suspicion that this was yet another part of their life he'd woefully neglected. 'Zeph…you didn't have to…'

'And yet I have,' he said gruffly.

She remained still as he fastened the necklace around her neck. And as he'd expected, it was perfect. But true perfection would come at the end of the night, when he set out his plans.

'Shall we?'

They went downstairs together, with Imogen glued to his side.

In the sea of faces that greeted them and the ensuing applause at his presence, Zeph searched shamelessly, frantic to find answers. A connection.

Nothing.

A stern-faced young man who dressed far too old for his age approached, pushing his boxy glasses up his nose. Zeph recognised him from their video calls.

'Spyros. Good of you to come.'

His assistant nodded, then proceeded to search Zeph's face.

Zeph gave a subtle shake of his head. 'No, nothing yet.'

Spyros's shoulders slumped a little.

With a tight smile, Zeph clasped him on the shoulder. 'Have faith, I'll be back before you know it.'

Surprise registered in his eyes before he managed to mask it. 'Yes, sir.'

'It's a party. Go and enjoy yourself.'

Advice he couldn't seem to take himself as he mingled with Imogen. Half of the guests he could barely tolerate, and the other half looked at him with a mixture of apprehension and awe.

A mere two hours later and he wanted them gone. Wanted nothing but Imogen and him, dancing to slow, haunting songs on a tiny pocket-square dance floor in the forgotten corner of a charming city.

Leaving yet another group of guests who swore they would bend over backwards should he need anything, he took Imogen's hand, raised it to his lips.

'How much longer?' he growled under his breath.

She cast a shrewd glance around before delivering an impish smile. 'One last surprise then you can kick everyone out if you wish.'

'I wish,' he confirmed immediately. 'Very much.'

She laughed.

And that single, musical sound, settling deep and sure, dictated his fate.

They might not have started at a place that pleased them both, but they could change course. Settle on a mutually pleasing path.

'Organise this surprise, *agape mou*. But do it quickly.'

Her smile held mocking long-suffering as she patted his chest. 'Your wish, my command. Give me five minutes.'

He watched her walk away, and although that ever-present ache lingered, Zeph could for the first time entertain the possibility that it would not stay for much longer. Perhaps even be alleviated once and for all tonight.

His gaze shifted to a guest whose name he couldn't recall. The man was making his way towards Zeph, his pregnant wife hanging on to his arm.

A new, breath-stealing pulse of need throbbed through him. *Imogen. Pregnant.*

He was thirty-five. With no family. Wasn't it time…?

He froze as the niggle at the back of his mind from earlier coalesced into knowledge. Into a kernel of a possibility, perhaps even a shape of his future.

By the time he focused, Imogen had disappeared into the crowd. He followed, the need to explore this possible new path driving him forward.

Halfway across one of the many living rooms cleared for guests to mingle, he heard her laugh. Felt his own lips curve in response.

Until he saw who his wife was laughing with. His smile disappeared, a sharp kick to his insides drawing a displeased grunt.

Imogen and the young, eager buck—Nate? Nick?—were heading for the rear of the house, and as they drifted from the music their voices carried.

'Are you considering going Stateside soon?' the man asked.

A shrug from Imogen. 'Maybe. We'll have to see how the next few months play out.'

'Give me a call when you do. I'd love to catch up.'

Was it the height of cliché to realise your entire world was wrapped up in one person just as some upstart attempted to snatch it away?

Because that was what Zeph felt in that moment.

And that was what he prowled forward, with purpose, to rectify.

CHAPTER NINE

'WE'LL HAVE TO *see how the next few months play out.*'

It hurt Imogen's soul to say the words to Noah.

Hurt even more that she had no clue what her own marriage held in store for her. Would Zeph forgive her if and when he regained his memories?

Would he still hold her to the six months once he remembered the true state of their marriage?

'Can I get you a drink?' Noah asked, noting her empty hands.

'I'll take care of it,' Zeph slid in smoothly from beside her, his voice clipped.

She glanced at him, confirmed that the voice matched the look on his face. 'Noah is resigning. He's got offers he claims he has to consider.' Her smile was bittersweet. She'd enjoyed working with him.

'Ah, then I'm sure there are other people you'd like to introduce yourself to now that you're window shopping.' From Zeph's tone of voice, one could easily swap *introduce* for *intrude.*

Noah took his cue from that and beat a hasty retreat.

'I'm not sure why you dislike him so much.'

His mouth twisted. 'Are you truly that oblivious?'

'What?'

'He's in love with you,' Zeph supplied, quiet fury brimming the words.

'What? No!'

His nostrils flared. 'It would probably crush him to hear your hot denial.'

Another tiny rip in her chest made her breath catch. 'Is he the one you care about?'

His eyes gleamed. 'I'm perfectly capable of ensuring your young puppy doesn't sniff around what's mine and also ensuring my wife isn't blind to what's happening around her.'

'Right. Consider me adequately warned.'

For the longest time, he held her gaze. When he nodded it was with pure masculine satisfaction and in the assurance that whatever message he wanted to give had been delivered.

And it had. Not that she needed it.

Because somewhere between falling into Zeph's bed and arriving in Italy, she'd lost the last ounce of fight where protecting her heart was concerned.

She was in love with her husband.

The rip turned into a tear, oozing panic and desperation. Old or new Zeph, she knew her feelings would most likely not be welcome. Just as she knew trying to contain them would rip her apart.

'I just left you. Did you want something?' she asked, striving to keep her voice even and a smile pinned on her face.

He opened his mouth, then at a bark of laughter from behind them, his jaw tightened. His gaze drifted over her, lingering on her belly and hips before, a fierce light in his eyes, he shook his head. 'Not now.'

'Okay. I need... I'll be right back. I need to check on a couple of things.'

He gave a brisk nod but didn't move. After a moment, she turned and hurried away, aware his gaze was pinned on her.

Had he seen? Did he know her fresh, raw feelings?

How could he when she'd only just discovered them herself?

But remember who you're dealing with.

Her panic escalated as the unnecessary checks were done, assurances given by the planner that all was in order.

Then she had no choice but to return to Zeph's side.

He took her hand immediately, openly kissing her knuckles before clamping a hand on her hip to keep her at his side.

Together they watched the spectacular fireworks over the lake before the strong hints that

Zeph wanted them gone quickly dispersed the guests.

When Apostolos deliberately straggled to catch Zeph's attention, and then skilfully cornered him, Imogen took the opportunity to seek another breather.

She'd already fallen into bed with a husband who hadn't wanted intimacy with her at the start of their marriage. How on earth would she manage to keep her love a secret when every look, every gesture made her heart ache and sing in the best and worst ways?

Like Zeph, she hadn't yet toured the house because she'd been too busy ensuring their guests would be fully catered for. So she was discovering darling little gems at every turn as she went through the villa now. Bypassing the organised chaos in the kitchen, she stumbled into a small, charming courtyard with a large olive-green door leading outside.

Two small benches were situated in front of a fountain, with a tidy vegetable patch on one side and a compact rose garden on the other.

She perched on the edge of one bench, her hands bunched in her lap. She was abstractly glad she wasn't freaking out on the outside because on the inside, Imogen reeled. Did she offer up her feelings and hope this new Zeph would welcome this…development?

She couldn't call it a gift because her love, so far in her life, had been seen as a burden.

Heart squeezing, she shut her eyes, only to open them again when the sound of heavy footsteps alerted her to Zeph's presence.

He prowled into the courtyard like a man with battle on his mind. Whether it was for her or against her was another matter.

His eyes zeroed in on her, and her heart thudded harder. 'Zeph…' she started, not really sure what came next. Her doom? Her ecstasy?

The hard shake of his head dried her attempt. 'Apostolos just told me some things. Things I would like answers—'

She stared at him as he suddenly froze. But he wasn't looking at her.

His gaze was fixed over her shoulder, his colour a sickly ash in the bright courtyard light.

'Zeph?'

A shiver-inducing sound ripped from his throat. Shaken, she turned to see what had provoked such a reaction. But there was nothing there.

She watched him stumble forward, his arm lifting to point. 'This. This is the door.'

Imogen gasped, her gaze whipping from his face to the door and back again. 'The door from your dreams? Are…are you sure?'

'Yes,' he breathed.

'H-how do you know?'

'Because I've lived that moment a million times. This was how my father would come in. He rarely used the front door because my mother was always in the kitchen with my grandmother. He would park the car around the back and come in that way. He would stop in town to pick up something because she was always forgetting some ingredient or other.'

His mouth twisted, his face a shattered painting. 'She was...impatient. He told me it was always best to appease her quickly if he wanted peace of mind.'

The eyes that rose to meet hers held a bottomless depth of bleakness.

'But you knew all of that. Didn't you?' he said with chilling finality.

And that icy condemnation in his voice?

It was pure Zephyr Diamandis.

The man she'd married almost two years ago.

'You remember!'

His face was a mask of cold, Stygian fury. 'Oh, yes, *dear wife*. I remember. Everything.'

Imogen willed herself to stop shivering. And failed.

She searched his face frantically for signs of softness. And failed to find any.

They'd relocated to the thankfully empty living room. By some unspoken signal the household and waitstaff had disappeared, leaving her alone with Zeph.

Who prowled back and forth in front of the giant fireplace like a caged animal.

'If you're struggling for somewhere to start, maybe I can help?' she offered, a desperate part of her wanting this to be over and done quickly so she could retreat to lick what wounds were inflicted. Because she knew they were coming.

Would she return to the States?

No. There was nothing left for her there. Hell, there was nothing left for her anywhere in the world. She'd dared to step out of her cold, lonely existence, to reach for light and warmth. Now she was about to be mercilessly flung back.

His hand slashing through the air stilled her frantic thoughts. 'I think you've done quite enough, don't you?'

'Have I? I'm sure you'll explain when you're ready.' She gave herself a little congratulatory pat for sounding remotely calm.

He stared her down from across the room, eyes like fired gems filled with accusation. 'You were quite clever, weren't you? You stormed into that church making me think you were reclaiming your husband. But you were saving yourself the inconvenience of having to wait around while I extricated myself from possibly bigamy?'

'Ah, I see we're back to that being my fault.'

'And you were very quick to inform me that my parents were dead. To intimate that I had no one else. No one besides you. You preyed on the off chance that I would want to keep you close. As my wife you were the natural, sensible choice to have at my side. Was that why you put up a token protest before agreeing to staying on the yacht? Because you didn't want me around anyone or anything that might trigger my memory returning?'

'What are you talking about? Where in all the things you've listed is my sin?'

'Your sin, dear wife, was not telling me that my so-called saviour was also my worst enemy. The daughter of the man directly responsible for me growing up with nothing!'

That shattered her cobbled-together calm. It pulverised her heart to unrecognisable pulp. But she had her voice. The fury in her soul. And she used them both.

'You know what? I expected all this.' She dashed away the shocked tears that filled her eyes, but more filled their place immediately. 'You were always going to find a way to blame me for everything. For not telling you about our rocky history. For what my family did to yours. Does it even matter to you that I was trying to protect you? That I didn't want to cause you pain for as long as I could prevent it?'

His head went back as if the very idea offended him. 'No. You knew about the door from my damned nightmares because I told you the first day you found me. And you said nothing because you were protecting yourself.'

'From what, exactly? From you thinking I was a gold-digger? As bad as or worse than my father and grandfather before me? I already knew that. You made it abundantly clear when you dragged me from America to a dingy little office in a town hall to marry me, then all but ignored me for the first year of our marriage.' Her voice threatened to crack. She held it together by sheer willpower, surging to her feet to meet him toe for toe.

'But the guy who I met in that church on Efemia? He had crumbs of decency about him. He smiled. He was courteous and considerate of other people. He *cared*. If you want me to think he was a figment of my imagination, fine. I'll wipe him from my memory. I'll pretend that the man who made love to me and brought me to tears of rapture doesn't exist, shall I? Go back to Athens, to your business acquaintances and everyone out there who hangs onto your every word and thinks you're Zeus reincarnated. I don't give a damn.'

A sound roared from him. Indecipherable and animal-like. A sound torn from his soul.

If he even had one?

Imogen was done trying to read this man. She'd relied on her emotions and got it wrong.

Hell, she'd done far worse.

She'd allowed herself to fall in love with a ghost. A fantasy replica of a monster.

'I saw you searching those faces tonight. And I know it hurt when you didn't find what you wanted. Believe me, I've had that all my life. But, Zeph, why won't you see what's right in front of you?'

'Another trick?'

Something shattered in her chest then. Her love might have been new and precious. But it was also deep and abiding. Until it'd twisted beneath his rejection.

'No. Not a trick. But I fear you won't recognise it until it's too late. Maybe never. You're just too blind. Your acolytes have paid their respects. You can sleep soundly tonight knowing you've been welcomed back with open arms.'

She turned away, heading blindly for the door. His cold voice stopped her.

'You're not walking away that easily. Not when there's the very real matter of you possibly carrying my child.'

Every cell in her body froze. 'What?'

'Last night, when we woke up in the middle of the night, we had sex. Without a condom. It skipped my mind until this evening.'

Her knees sagged and she reached for the nearest chair back.

They'd both been half asleep, had reached for each other with that blind, all-consuming hunger that sparked to life with very little effort on their parts and had fallen into a wild coupling that had left them panting for breath in the aftermath. It'd been glorious.

And it might be the one mistake that would spell her doom.

'Okay, thanks for letting me know,' she managed to bite out.

'Excuse me?' he roared.

She lifted her chin. 'You heard me. I'm not going to stand here and let you denigrate my character any longer. You're probably looking for a way to blame me for the lack of protection, too. Go back to Athens, Zeph. Do your worst. It's not like I'm not used to it. I'm sure you'll let me know the consequences of my actions in due course.'

She whirled away from him.

He caught her wrist, detaining her. 'Don't walk away from me, Imogen. We're not done.'

'You may not be. But I am. I'm tired of being everyone's punching bag. No more, Zeph. *No more.*'

His face slackened for a nanosecond before he caught himself. Reasserting that formidable tycoon aura that left men quaking.

But she was done shaking in her shoes for this man. She was done, period. 'What are you going to do, Zeph? Take Callahan from me? Go ahead. I fought for it because it was the last real thing that meant family to me. But it was just a pipe dream. I never really had much of a family for you to ruin in the first place.'

He held her gaze for several long moments, before his eyes dropped deliberately to her belly. As he'd done earlier this evening.

'What about the family you might be carrying? Does that not matter to you either? If not, I'd like that in writing so there's no dispute when the time comes.'

She gasped, the blood draining from her head when she grasped his meaning. 'When the time... You'd take a child away from its mother?'

'I'd fight heaven and earth to keep what's mine. As I always have.'

The words flayed her open, but she was damned if she would let him see her gaping wounds. 'Don't hide behind double meanings. Say what you mean.'

'Very well. If you are carrying my child, then you won't be going anywhere. Forget six months. Forget three-year agreements. Our marriage will be permanent. Is that plain enough for you?'

'Yes, I understand. Welcome back, Zeph. And

congratulations. You're officially still a Grade A monster.'

He nodded as if taking it as his rightful due. 'But I'm a monster who gets what he wants. And what he wants is for his wife to return to Athens with him in the morning. You will smile and cling to my every word. Because, baby or no baby, Imogen, we're still married. And you still have an agreement to fulfil.'

In all corners of his life, Zeph relished being proved right. A well-placed 'I told you so' was even warranted here and there, when a point needed driving home further.

Right in this moment, he wished every one of his senses to hell for the repeated warnings he'd hoped wouldn't come true. For the suspicion that whatever Imogen was withholding from him would be monumental. For the even greater suspicion that only she held the key to freeing him from the haunting loneliness in his life.

The bone-deep addiction to her. And not just to her body. Her beautiful mind, her generous spirit.

And that unmoored sensation he'd suspected wouldn't go away even when he regained his memories.

He despised every last one of those revelations.

Because it meant in this most important battle of his life, he would not win. Unless…unless…

'Spyros!'

His PA rushed in, his features tense. *Ne*, he was setting everyone around on edge. And he wasn't entirely sure he was sorry. A problem shared and all that.

But he wanted to share his problem with only one person.

'Where is my wife?' he demanded without looking up.

When she'd thrown that livid 'like hell I will' at him two weeks ago after he'd ordered her back to Athens, he'd laughed, certain she wouldn't be so foolish as to call his bluff.

Well, she'd called it. She'd left. Then turned the dark light of his life a new shade of obsidian with a simple text a few days later.

I'm not pregnant.

He hadn't believed he could locate a lower level of desolation until that text had arrived.

His eyes felt scratchy, and he was sure they were bloodshot. The headache Imogen was so adept at soothing was pounding at his temples, a relentless reminder of what he'd thrown away.

Theós, he needed her, dammit!

You know what you have to do.

He released a low growl when Spyros continued to remain silent. 'Did you not hear me? I asked where my—'

'She asked that her whereabouts not be disclosed to you, sir.'

He sucked in a deep breath. 'What?' he bellowed.

'I'm sorry, sir.'

'I don't want an apology. I want to know where my wife is,' he breathed, fury boiling in his stomach. How dared she disappear when... when...?

He froze. Dear God, was she paying him back for leaving her for almost a year?

No. The woman he'd spent the last several weeks with wouldn't do that.

She wasn't...

He surged to his feet, unable to contain the growing realisation that he might have got a lot of things wrong. 'Spyros,' he tried again, striving to keep his voice steady. He failed. Cringed when he heard it crack right down the middle. 'Tell me where my wife is.'

He suspected he'd hit rock bottom when his assistant stared at him with something eerily close to pity. 'I don't know, sir. But...might I suggest you explore the possibility of device-tracking with your head of security?' Spyros said.

Zeph was lunging for his phone when the other man calmly exited and shut the door.

Scotland.

His wife was in Scotland. Upon hearing it, he'd panicked and instructed his security to look into who his wife was staying with. Why, of all the places she could've fled to, she'd chosen the rugged but unwelcoming Highlands. Of course, he'd felt like a heel for believing her capable of that too.

But had that stopped him from jumping on his jet and chasing her down?

Absolutely not.

That was not to say he wasn't in a foul mood by the time he located the love of his life, striding down the side of a mountain with fire brimming in her eyes as she glared at his departing helicopter. The majority of the foulness was directed at himself though. It would be for a very long time, he suspected.

'What are you doing here?'

Zeph knew poets wrote reams about this place, and, while the rolling mountains were decent enough, in his eyes the woman standing in front of him was the most beautiful sight he'd ever seen.

The russet hair that had gained highlights during their time on the yacht glinted beneath the Highland sun, and her face glowed with health and beauty. Did it disgruntle him a little that she looked so spectacular when he was suffering? Maybe. But he deserved that too.

'I could ask you the same question. Why here?'

She shrugged her despondency, leaving him a fraction more desolate, a feat he wouldn't have believed was possible before it happened. 'I don't have a company any more so I'm thinking of becoming a sheep farmer. What do you care?'

He sucked in a long breath. 'Did you think placing an infuriating number of mountains between us was going to stop me coming after you?'

'I don't care. Just…please, go away.'

The sliver of desperation in her voice triggered another spark in him. Because he recognised it as his own, multiplied by a million. But her desperation didn't mean she was experiencing similar feelings. Perhaps it was because he'd burned every last component in the bridge leading back to her.

'How did you even find me?' she cried when she realised he wasn't going to budge.

Did she know he was incapable of it? Taking a step away from her would end him. 'I used every resource I had at my disposal and I don't apologise for it.'

She opened her mouth to condemn him some more.

But he hurried to speak before she could. 'I had

to find you, *agape mou.*' He shook his head. 'I fought an ocean and survived but I've come to realise that I won't survive you not taking me back, Imogen. *Parakalo.* Please hear me out?' There was that infuriating crack in his voice again.

Out here in this frigid middle of nowhere for the sheep to hear. They bleated their indifference as his wife's eyes widened.

She'd heard it too no doubt. Was readying to send him away for the fool he was.

His breath tangled in his lungs when she took a step. But it wasn't away from him, it was towards him.

His hands shook at his sides, every fibre of his being fighting to remain still and not reach out for her.

'No. Please go away,' she repeated. 'I don't want you here.'

His heart lurched but he bounced back almost immediately. 'I don't want to be here either.'

She stiffened, her nose tilting upward in that affronted way that made him want to sweep her into his arms. 'You shouldn't have sent your pilot away, then. No matter, the road to town is that way.' She pointed over his shoulder.

'I don't want to be here because I want us both back on that yacht with nothing between us but laughter. And conversation. And sex.'

Her eyes clung for a moment before dismissing him again. 'That was a dream. A few weeks suspended in time until the real you came back. Remember?'

He flinched. 'The real me.' He laughed. 'I don't know who or what that is any more.'

She hesitated and he snatched at the opportunity.

'How can I still be the man hell-bent on revenge when without you I would still be lost?'

Imogen shook her head. 'You would've regained your memories eventually. It was only a matter of—'

'I don't mean my lost memories, Imogen. I mean myself. The man I am here.' He thumped at his heart. 'You showed me who I was without me even knowing I was on a journey of discovery. You opened my eyes to better, far better than I'd ever known, *agape mou*.'

She nodded wretchedly. 'Oh, yes. I did all of that. And you still threw me away. So easily.'

His throat closed and he had to swallow several times before he could speak. 'I was terrified how much I craved you. All my life I've relied on no one but myself. The family I loved was taken from me in the blink of an eye. I had to learn to exist as a lone wolf. I held you at arm's length when we married because I didn't know any other way to exist. I've lived with loneliness and anger for so long, I couldn't separate the fact that your father and grandfather were the ones responsible, not every Callahan that lived and breathed.'

He gritted his teeth, despising himself but unable to stop confessing the truth. 'Maybe I picked you to fulfil that agreement because I was envious that you'd had a family when I'd not. It was wrong but I wanted you to have a…taster of what I went through. And then you came and reclaimed me in that church. I suddenly…belonged to someone. I was falling in love with someone. I was no longer alone. It felt incredible. And far too good to be true. So I pushed it away. I pushed you away. For that, I will always regret it and beg your forgiveness.'

Her mouth dropped open. 'Y-you're in love with…me?'

'So, so much.' Admitting it felt…sublime. Like a second…third rebirth. 'After the party, I planned to ask you to forget the agreement, the stupid six months. Everything. I said once that I should marry you again. I meant it then although the delivery could've been better. Maybe I sensed deep down that I'd gone about it the wrong way the first time.'

'Zeph…you love me?' she repeated, her eyes filling with tears.

He ventured close, despising the wind that picked up, whipping her hair into her face so he couldn't see her beautiful eyes. When she lifted her hand to tuck her hair away, he saw the wedding rings still on her finger. And it almost dropped him to his knees.

'I love you, Imogen Diamandis. It took the gift of memory loss for me to discover that I couldn't live without you. If you take me back I vow to never leave your side. Bind me to your side and let me love you until the world stops turning. Please.'

She burst into tears. He scooped her up and held her to his heart, this treasure he'd so foolishly discarded. Twice. The shock of that near loss made him seek her lips, to rabidly reaffirm and reawaken the heart he'd feared would stop beating without her.

And his heart soared when she kissed him back.

When they parted, she passed a despondent hand over her stomach. 'I'm sorry the pregnancy test was negative. I didn't know how much I wanted to be pregnant until I was not.'

We can fix that. Immediately.

He swallowed the words before they damned him. He still had a lot of work to do. One of those chilly mountains to climb. 'That's the way hard lessons are learnt, isn't it? Denying what's right in front of us until it's taken away. Then we're exposed for the utter fools we are.'

'You did *not* just call me a fool,' she threw back,

her beautiful eyes snapping with fire. And something else that made his heart stutter with hope.

'Oh, no, *agape mou*. That honour is reserved only for me.'

Something leapt in those eyes he adored so much. 'You can call yourself all the names in the world. As long as you keep loving me half as much as I love you.'

His grateful, triumphant roar scared the sheep, who went scattering across the hills. He didn't care. Or he cared only if Imogen did.

Right now, all he wanted to do was kiss her again.

So he did. Until they were both breathless and clinging to one another.

'I need you, *agape mou*. As for Callahan, I fear I have a mini mutiny on my hands. None of the clients are happy dealing with me. They want you back. Hell, even my board have been overheard saying you're a much more amenable CEO to deal with than me.'

'Only because they think they can call the shots.'

He dropped a long kiss on her lips. 'Not any more. They dragged their feet but forcing them to admit how invaluable you've been in my absence has made them see the light. Diamandis needs you back. *I* need you back, Imogen. By my side, where you belong. I've been entirely miserable without you.'

'Oh, Zeph. Me too.'

He looked around and grimaced. 'As much as I would like to seal our love immediately, I don't think I can quite reduce myself to seducing you with the sheep watching.'

She laughed, and his heart soared.

When it came close to settling, Zeph realised that the ache had evaporated. Accepting love, opening his own heart in return, had healed them both.

He wanted to drop to his knees in humbled thanksgiving. But his wife had other ideas. When her hand snuck beneath his coat, searching, caressing, his breath caught.

'I'm renting a cottage about a mile away,' she murmured against his lips.

Zeph's heart, and other parts of his needy body, jumped, even as he shook his head and reached into his pocket. 'I have a better idea. I can have our chopper here in two minutes.'

She gasped. 'I thought you sent him away?'

'Only over the hill. Your husband is no fool. I will buy you this mountain if you desire, but for what I have in mind we will need solid walls and indoor plumbing.'

She laughed again, flinging her arms around his neck.

'I can't wait for our next adventure to start, Zeph. I love you.'

His throat closed. Again. And it took until the rotors of his helicopter drew near for him to reply. 'I was lost, and you found me. You saved me, my love. I belong to you now, *eros mou*. For ever.'

* * * * *

If you got lost in the passion of
The Greek's Forgotten Marriage,
then why not dive into these other
Maya Blake stories?

Reclaimed for His Royal Bed
Bound by Her Rival's Baby
A Vow to Claim His Hidden Son
Their Desert Night of Scandal
His Pregnant Desert Queen

Available now!